When Love Finds Me

EXPANDED EDITION

TYORA MOODY

TYMM PUBLISHING

When Love Finds Me

A Novella

Chapter One

I hated when I did this to myself, but I couldn't stop glancing at the clock. It wasn't like I could control the clock's hands with my sheer will. Today, Crown of Beauty Salon hummed with a steady flow of clients. I had two regulars this morning and I decided to accommodate a mid-morning walk-in, whose hair I carefully hurried to finish now. The walk-in used to be a regular client I hadn't seen in months. Miss Claire Rowell was a sweet older woman on a fixed income and there was no way I could turn her away. As I pulled the rollers from her hair, I tried deep breathing as best I could without being obvious. My anxiety levels were at an all-time high due to barely getting two hours of sleep last night.

Girlfriend, you need to get a grip.

I, Tangerine Nelson, just Tangie to most, had been the co-owner of the salon for about six months, ever since the former co-owner officially retired to care for her ailing husband. I'd been working at the salon for about eight years prior to the ownership change, the longest I'd ever worked anywhere. I loved what I did and the salon founder was one of my dearest friends. Candace Jackson knew what it meant to me to become a partner. Lately, I felt like I was destroying the partnership as well as our friendship. Today, Candace had been gracious once again about me taking time off.

I sighed deeply as I began styling Miss Rowell's hair, determined not to look at the clock. Calculating in my head, I knew I had an hour to make it on time to my afternoon appointment... *if* Charlotte's traffic wouldn't hold me up. It was almost two o'clock in the afternoon but it had been my experience that there was really no time of the day when cars were not an issue on I-77.

As if she could sense my turmoil, Candace showed up at my side. "Hey, Tangie, how are you doing? If you need me to finish up Miss Rowell's hair, let me know."

"No, I got it." I glanced at Candace via the mirror. "Thanks for the offer. I appreciate it."

Candace patted me on the shoulder. "Okay, see me before you leave. I will be taking care of paperwork in the office."

I nodded and then immediately regretted glancing at the clock. It was now five minutes after two o' clock.

How did that happen?

Miss Rowell smiled appreciatively as she patted her silvery hairstyle, promising to return in the near future. I gratefully accepted her extra tip for the roller set and despite my anxious-filled day was pleased by my elderly client's joy. As I headed back to the office, I slipped out of my purple salon vest. The vests were my idea a few years back. The logo for Crown of Beauty was emblazoned on the right side. I actually sketched it myself, an outline of a woman with glorious curls around the top of her head, like a crown. Long time employees like myself also had our names embossed under the logo.

I hung the vest on a hook behind the office door, and then moved swiftly to the other side of the room to open the closet door. My large brown bag sat on the floor. I lifted it and dug inside for my car keys. With keys in hand, I started to leave but then suddenly remembered Candace's request.

"Did you want to see me?" I asked, whirling back around to face the desk where Candace sat.

Candace stopped typing on the computer. "Yes, I wanted to pray with you. If that's okay. I know you're in a hurry, but it has been a busy morning with you accommodating the walk-in."

My shoulders slumped.

I *was also late this morning too.* Candace was gracious enough not to mention, instead offering me prayer.

"Girl, I'm not turning down prayer. I don't regret the walk-in. Miss Rowell is a blessing to me. She was really excited about getting to travel to her family reunion in Charleston. Poor lady doesn't get out much these days."

Candace stepped around the desk, a wide grin spread across our face. "You know my policy is not to turn anyone away if we can fit them in. We take care of our elderly ladies in this shop because we are never too old to stop looking good."

Candace grabbed my hands and I closed my eyes. This salon office had become a meeting room for prayer so many times, especially in the past few months.

"Let's pray." Candace began, "*Lord, we ask for protection and safety for Tangie as she heads down the road. We pray that you provide her peace beyond all understanding as she and her baby boy take on this new venture. We know that you opened the doors for Drake and that you intend for him to thrive. Help Tangie to continue to trust you and put her faith in you. You know what's best and will work out all things for their good. We ask these in Jesus name we pray. Amen."*

I took a breath, feeling the release that had been pressuring me all day. I never considered myself a woman who could cry so easily, but in the past few years as my sons have grown up before my eyes, I found that leaning on God was the only thing that kept me from falling apart. I've been a single mom for so long and I often needed to be reminded I wasn't alone. That I could let my burdens go.

I grabbed tissues from the desk and wiped the moisture from my eyes. "Thank you, I appreciate your prayers and your patience too. I know I haven't been able to pull myself fully into this partnership and I haven't pulled my weight with clients."

Candace shook her head. "Don't worry. I've been there with my two children. They are both grown now, but as a mother, you never stop worrying, especially when life is not treating your child in a good way. This all will pass, Tangie."

I knew I could trust Candace's testimony. She'd lost her husband ten years ago and raised her children alone before remarrying her current husband. I'd always admired Candace's journey from her grief and loss. It was crazy how both of her husbands were in law enforcement. Despite the fears, I knew my friend lived a life dependent on faith.

Was it even possible for me to have a strong godly man in my life?

I had that kind of man in my life once. But now my life was dedicated to my boys.

"Thank you, again. I appreciate your friendship more than I can ever express."

We shared a quick hug before I hurried outside towards my car. After I cranked the ignition on my Toyota Sienna, I welcomed the cool blast of air on my face. I typed the address to where I was heading into the van's GPS screen. This van was not my dream car, but it had served me well over the years. Unfortunately it also looked and smelled like the three boys I often transported to various activities. My boys kept me up at night and it wasn't because they were bad kids. I'd been blessed with some talented young men, but this weekend, they would all be tasked with vacuuming and washing the van.

As I headed out the parking lot adjacent to the salon, I had to smile at the thought of my rambunctious boys, almost young men, with the garden hose, probably going at each other with the water instead of concentrating on their chore.

I sighed deeply recalling a conversation with the twins about getting another car. One of the reasons I was excited about the partnership at the salon, it allowed me to put aside money for an extra car. Both twins had their driver's permits. Although I was not ready for them to be driving, this mama needed a break. I knew I had to let go for my own sanity and allow these boys their independence.

When my mama was alive she always told me girls were hard. I guess that was because her experience was raising three girls, with me being the youngest. My sisters and I all managed to get pregnant at young ages, just like my mother. My pregnancy at age seventeen seemed to wound her the most. She felt like I should have learned from my two older sisters.

When we found out I was going to have twins, Mama put aside her disappointment to help me. I walked with my class for graduation, big belly and all. Later, I finished up my cosmetology degree, but instead of working at a salon, I spent years working in retail at various department stores, occasionally offering braids and hair extension services on the side to earn extra cash.

I merged into traffic on I-77, thinking of my younger days. My life had changed so much. Now at age thirty-three, I felt more grounded. Despite being a single mom, my life was full. Martin, the oldest twin by three minutes, was the point guard for South Meck High School's basketball team during his sophomore year. My boy was good, no doubt, but I worried about how much his high school fame was going to his head. He was a good-looking kid too. His twin Mark, not as athletic but more book smart, was also devastatingly handsome. Mark played in the marching band with the goal of becoming a drum major. My high-achieving twins stayed glued to their phones, which I knew were filled with texts from girls. I lived on edge, sometimes borderline fear for my twins who turned sixteen a few weeks ago. They were growing into men far earlier than I was ready.

What I didn't expect was the nightmare that entered my baby boy's life this past school year. Drake was only ten years old. Unlike the twins,

Drake was quiet, incredibly sweet and a little on the chubby side. I had to get him fitted for near-sighted glasses when he was in first grade. My little nerd! The boy read anything, including an old set of encyclopedias my mother had bought when I was in school. While I worried about the twins and what they were doing on their phones, I was never disappointed when I checked Drake's tablet. He was more than likely reading a book. I admired him for that and often wished I possessed his appetite for reading.

The woman's voice from the navigation system broke through my thoughts.

In two miles, take exit 13 towards I-85.

I gripped the steering wheel as I caught sight of the traffic ahead. Cars seemed to be moving steadily, but there was still too much traffic. I glanced at the dashboard clock and gritted my teeth. Almost two-thirty. I couldn't afford to be late.

Drake was the last one I would ever expect to get into trouble in school. The call from Smithfield Elementary took me by sheer surprise. My sweet boy got into a fight. Sent home for a five day suspension. Five whole days. This kid had never been in trouble before.

It took me three days to drag out of him what prompted the fight.

"That boy has been bothering me for months, Mama." Drake eyes were sad, but defiant, "I was tired of him. No one was listening to me. When he hit me, I'd had enough."

Bullying! I was stunned. *Why didn't someone tell me?*

Come to find out he'd told his teacher, the school counselor and the principal. Nobody did anything. No one bothered to call me. Well, until it was too late.

When I asked Drake why he didn't tell me, he just shrugged.

That shrug hurt. I felt like out of all the adults I'd failed my son the most.

Drake had always been the quietest. He never complained. Ever. I took that as a good sign. But it wasn't good. When Drake was younger he could babble for hours, asking questions. As he got older, he still had questions, but he learned how to read and find answers on his own.

I admit when I found out about the bullying, I didn't handle the meeting with the principal very well. I could tell within a few minutes of talking to the man that he was a condescending jerk, who had already labeled my son a troublemaker for the fight. He didn't care that my son was defending himself from a bully who threw the first punch. The fact that my son reported the bullying months before didn't seem to faze the principal nor did it stop the suspension.

I knew I needed to do something.

Drake's brothers were six years older and there never was a time when all the boys were at the same school. I'd often wondered if the bullying would have been an issue if Martin and Mark were around.

I had to reboot Drake for success. He was too smart to let an incident like this take him down. Some ladies from Victory Gospel Church, where I attended, suggested several charter schools in the area. And after researching and visiting open houses, I applied to the Charlotte STEM Lab School, also known as "The Lab." Their application system was based on a lottery, but I trusted God that Drake's name would be selected.

I was so overjoyed last Monday for the call and immediately told Drake. His face spoke volumes, his anxiety evident. During the spring, he had returned to school after the suspension, walking on eggshells. His grades had suffered from the stress. Drake never made less than a B, but ended up with two Cs on his final report card.

We needed this school to work for him.

It didn't help my anxiety when I received another call at the end of last week, this time from the school counselor. He wanted me to make an appointment to talk about Drake. The call was ominous and had wreaked havoc on my nervous system the entire weekend until now.

What did the counselor want? Was he going to hold Drake's suspension against him and not let him into the school?

School started in three weeks and I had set my hopes on The Lab. It's promises of challenge-based learning, science and technology was what I knew Drake needed.

I guided the van towards the exit and after a few turns, the navigation system led me into the school's parking lot. It was a modern building with a manicured landscape around the front. I took another breath and prayed again before stepping out of the van. When I swung open the school doors, I was consumed by the quietness of the building, with no students or faculty. I headed towards the glass windows where I spotted a bronze sign on the wall.

Administration.

I swung open the dark mahogany door and stepped inside, the royal blue carpeting with its zig zag pattern caught my attention before I looked up. A woman who looked close to my age sat at a desk behind the counter. She glanced up from the computer monitor and smiled. "May I help you?"

I stepped forward, steeling myself for whatever lay ahead in this meeting. "Yes, my son will be starting school here in a few weeks and I have an appointment with Nathan Chambers."

"Wait one moment." The woman swiveled around to pick up the phone on her desk. "Nathan, you have a parent here to see you."

I sat down, admiring the woman's hair. She wore goddess locs, and they were well done. I was still the only stylist at our salon who specialized in doing braids and locs. I reserved these clients for Fridays and Saturdays since the process took a while. I used to wear them myself. So much had changed with how I kept up with my looks and fashion. I couldn't remember the last time I had a manicure or a pedicure, something I used to do quite regularly. There was no time these days.

"Mrs. Nelson?"

A smooth baritone voice interrupted my thoughts of how my life used to be. I glanced up and then found myself gripping the arms of the chair for a moment. I recognized the voice from the phone call last week, but what I didn't realize was who the voice was attached to.

When did school counselors start looking like this?

Nathan Chambers was a gorgeous chocolate brother. Perfect white teeth. And beautiful brown eyes... eyes that were looking at me with some concern.

I know I was freaking out on the way here, but this is something entirely different. Pull it together, Tangie.

I blinked and stood, embarrassed by whatever came over my senses. I reached for the man's outstretched hand. "Mr. Chambers?" I said the man's name a bit breathier than I usually spoke. It was like something snuck up on me and snatched the wind out of my lungs.

He smiled, "Yes, I'm the middle school counselor here. I'm happy you were able to meet with me this afternoon. Follow me, my office is this way."

"Okay." I gripped my hands at my sides as I followed Mr. Chambers back towards his office. I'm not really sure how I made it back there, because my mind had drifted to places it hadn't crossed in years.

Chapter Two

I couldn't recall the last time I felt this way. My face felt warm and tingly, like someone had turned up the temperature in the building. I had to physically pinch myself as I sat across from Mr. Chambers. Seriously, I was ogling the man. He was a beautiful man with the kind of sculpted looks you see on a celebrity or ran across in your Instagram feed. I wouldn't call him pretty. Definitely manly.

Does he workout? He has to because that white shirt is perfectly molded. ...Stop it, Tangie!

I couldn't believe my reaction to this man in front of me. And of all times. Right now! Shameful! I was here to talk about my son, to put that nightmare of a school year we just had behind us.

I was a godly Christian single mom, raising three boys, and I was a successful business woman.

That man-crazy woman I used to be ... she was gone. She had disappeared a long time ago. That woman never recovered from the pain of loss.

I pinched myself again when I found Mr. Chambers staring at me again. I gulped, at this point not even sure if the man had said something to me or not. "I'm sorry if I seem a bit flustered to you, but I was so excited about Drake being accepted here and your phone call threw me for a loop. Is something wrong?"

Mr. Chambers shook his head, his smile reassuring, "No need to worry. We set up appointments with parents for all students who are new to The Lab."

"Okay, so this isn't some kind of preliminary test? I mean Drake's application was selected through the lottery process. I know you have his school records from his previous school. He's a really smart boy."

"Yes, he is. I have looked over his school records. I believe The Lab will be a perfect learning environment for Drake."

"But..." Whatever hormonal foolishness going through my head a few moments ago was replaced by the anxiety that plagued me the past few days.

"Mrs. Nelson, you don't have to worry," Mr. Chambers held out his hands towards me, as if he wanted to calm me down.

They were nice hands. Long fingers, well-manicured fingernails.

Lord, what is wrong with me?

I took a deep breath and leaned forward in the chair. "Look, I really prayed for Drake to be accepted here. He was bullied at his last school. Not one of the adults stepped up to help him. In hindsight, I wish I had known or saw signs, but even I didn't know what was going on with him. He tried to defend himself and he was punished. He needs this fresh start. He's a brilliant boy."

I sat back in the chair, a bit exhausted from my tirade.

Mr. Chambers watched me, probably wondering if I was the one he should be worried about. After what felt like a very long few seconds, he asked, "Do you have other children, Mrs. Nelson?"

I frowned. "Yes, I have two older boys, twins. They attend South Meck. Good boys. All of my boys are good."

Mr. Chambers smiled, "I'm sure they are. They have a passionate mother determined that they achieve their best. I admire that. I'm where I am now because of a really strong mom determined to make sure I succeeded."

He sat back in his chair. "Like I said, you have no worries. The board did note the suspension on Drake's record, but we also saw that he wasn't in trouble any time before then and after. I appreciate you explaining the circumstances he was under at his previous school. We can't guarantee that type of incident won't come up again, but I can assure you if a student comes to me about any sort of bullying, I will make sure to nip it in the bud right away."

That made me smile, and I felt the tension melt from my body. "Thank you, I appreciate that. Please let me know how I can be more involved."

"Certainly, The Lab needs volunteers all the time. We have a vibrant PTO. I will be sure to share that information before the end of our meeting. In the meantime, I'd like to go over the schedule that we have for Drake."

He handed me a set of stapled papers across the desk. I reached for them, grateful to be able to focus my attention anywhere except Mr. Chambers' face.

I read along while Mr. Chambers explained Drake's classes and structure of his daily schedule. The man's voice soothed my nerves.

"He's definitely gifted and I believe the curriculum will challenge him in ways that he needs and also desires. This year we're starting a robotics program. How do you think Drake would feel about being involved?"

Now I couldn't keep the smile off my face if I tried. I lifted my head to face Mr. Chambers. "That sounds wonderful. He will be so excited."

"Good, I look forward to meeting Drake. He's going to do great here at The Lab. If you need anything or want to come in to discuss Drake, feel free. We encourage parents to be involved with their children's learning. Even though Drake is entering middle school, this is the time of his life when he needs even more guidance."

Mr. Chambers stood and reached out his hand.

I stood as well, to shake his hand. For a second it seemed like we held each other's hands a bit longer than necessary. In fact, I'm pretty sure I let go first.

Mr. Chambers came from around the desk to walk me out. Now, I'm a tall woman, five foot eight, but Mr. Chambers appeared to tower over me. I didn't notice this when I followed him to his office, probably because I was observing his backside.

Shameful, Tangie!

I had no idea what possessed me, but I asked, "Did you play basketball? No offense, I just had to ask. You have to be at least six foot four or five."

He grinned, "I get that question a lot, and nice guess! Six foot five and I did play at South Meck back in the day. Couple of state championships. Later, I played at UNC."

"Wow! My son is a point guard for South Meck."

"Really? Wait," he looked at me as if he was thinking hard about something. "Nelson. Your son is Martin Nelson?"

"That's my boy." I knew I was beaming.

"Small world. A couple of my buddies were talking about him. He's really talented."

"Thank you. I found it hard to believe when he told me he made varsity last year. I hoped it wouldn't go completely to his head."

Mr. Chambers let out a deep throaty laugh. "I was placed on varsity when I was a sophomore too. It's quite the ego boost for a teenage boy."

I sighed, "I've seen the effects."

Mr. Chambers reached back to his desk and grabbed a business card. He wrote on the back of the card. "Here's my card. If you have any issues, not just with Drake. If you need a friendly talk from a guy for one of your other sons, I mentor outside of school. That's my personal cell on the back of the card."

"Thank you, Mr. Chambers."

"Nathan. Please call me Nathan."

I looked up at those eyes again thinking this was definitely not how I saw this meeting going at all. "Okay, friends call me Tangie."

"It was nice to meet you, Tangie. I hope to see you again."

As I stepped outside of Mr. Chambers, uhm, Nathan's office, I realized I wanted to see him again too.

Chapter Three

After church on Sunday, my longtime friend and mentor, Beulah Samuels invited us to her house for dinner. Beulah worked at Crown of Beauty for years before retiring a year ago. She was the backbone of the salon, being the oldest stylist in the house. I loved how Beulah didn't let her age stop her from being stylish, and I missed her dearly. The older woman was the life of the salon, bringing good humor and plenty of good gossip. She knew everybody and everybody knew her.

Now more important things filled her life. Harold Samuels had been displaying signs of dementia for some time and became the reason why Beulah finally retired from the beauty business she loved. I hadn't seen Beulah in a few weeks and

I knew under her bubbly exterior, she was lonely taking care of her husband.

When I entered Beulah's home, with my three boys in tow, it felt like entering home. My mama passed away five years ago, and I missed her. She'd been my rock and the one I leaned on when my boys needed care due to my work hours. But she'd gone downhill in health as the boys grew older. Her battle with colon cancer was quick and dealt a brutal blow.

Beulah had filled in as a mother figure in so many ways. I welcomed any time she had for me and the boys. Since her and Harold never had children, I knew she loved to dote on us. When I told her about the boys starting back to school and Drake's new school, she wanted to make something special. Beulah loved to cook anytime of the year, no matter the occasion.

"Girl, look at you. I'm loving the new do." Beulah reached up and hugged me.

I grinned, "I decided to give the braids a break." I was enjoying my natural curls.

"Well, it looks good. You see what I've done to mine."

Beulah was sporting a short, silver cut with curls on the top, tapering into a fade down the sides and back.

"Miss Beulah, you always look good."

She turned her attention to my boys. "So how y'all doing? Give me my hugs."

Each of my loud and boisterous boys seemed to turn shy, but they all reached down and hugged Miss Beulah. It wasn't until I observed Drake bend a bit that I really noticed my baby had gained more inches than I realized over the summer. Even some of his baby fat seemed to have melted. The realization took my breath away for a moment.

I caught Beulah watching me. She lifted her eyebrow. "Are you doing okay?"

I waved my hand like I hadn't just received a shock. "Yeah, sure. We can catch up later. I know these younguns are starving."

Beulah eyed me a bit longer before heading into the kitchen.

The Sunday meal consisted of some of Beulah's specialties: fried chicken, collard greens, macaroni and cheese. I can't say it bothered me that this was the first real home-cooked meal my family had in a few weeks. I was not a bad cook, I just plain didn't have time to cook. Seemed like during the summer with the longer daylight hours, I spent more time in the salon. Plus my boys were old enough to feed themselves. I tried to use the slow-cooker some weekends. I even cooked and stored food in the freezer. There was currently a lasagna in the freezer that I'd planned to take out today as a backup. Now it could wait until after the boys started back to school.

As we served ourselves, passing around plates, I couldn't help but notice Beulah appeared more worn down than the last time I saw her. Harold was also at the table today. He had always been a quiet man, but today he appeared even older too. His head was almost bald with a slight sheen of silver hair. He sat stooped over his plate, occasionally smiling at everyone.

"Are you boys ready for school to start tomorrow?" Beulah asked.

Martin and Mark answered in grunts, with their heads both down in their plates. Thank goodness Drake remembered his manners. He grinned at Beulah and answered, "Yes, ma'am. This chicken is so good, Miss Beulah."

Beulah threw her head back and laughed. "Thank you, baby. Get some more if you want. I made plenty since I knew I had growing boys coming to dinner."

I had to smile because Drake's enthusiasm was infectious and also warmed my heart. He'd been talking about his upcoming first day at the new school all weekend. I hated to admit my mind lingered on more than just Drake's new school, but also his school counselor.

It had been a loooooong time since a man caught my eye. I was ashamed to admit. Years!

Since our meeting, I googled Nathan Chambers, doing what I classified as research. Nathan, as he insisted I call him, was going to be counseling my baby boy. With the influence he would have, in my mind, there was nothing wrong about checking out his background. A basketball star in both high school and college, Nathan had a very brief stint in the NBA with the New York Knicks. It was a shame a knee injury left him unable to fulfill a longer career in the NBA.

I almost sent him a friend request on Facebook. I pondered clicking the button for a whole fifteen minutes before my senses kicked in.

I was a grown woman with children. Not a stalker!

While I wasn't courageous enough to send a friend request, I didn't hesitate to follow his Instagram feed. Instagram made it so easy as long as people kept their profiles public. If Nathan happened to notice I followed him, I hoped he would think it was harmless. It wasn't like I had some sexy photo of myself.

Now back in the day in my early twenties, I probably would have, but my Instagram photo displayed me with my boys. It was an old photo. At the time Martin and Mark were ten and Drake was only four. Most of the photos on my feed were of my sons. If Nathan wanted to explore my Instagram, he would see I was a very devoted mother.

I think what attracted me to Nathan was his bounce back from basketball. It was nice to see an attractive, successful black man working inside a school. Almost rare in an environment dominated by white females.

After we devoured the meal, I helped Beulah clear the table and then clean the kitchen. As I loaded the dishwasher, Beulah asked, "How are you doing, Tangie? You've been quiet today."

"Oh. I didn't realize. Maybe I'm just nervous about tomorrow. I know Drake will do well in the new school. I just don't want a repeat of what happened last year."

"Well, you know bullies have been around since the beginning of time. Even adults have to deal with bullies."

"I know, but I'm happy I moved him from *that* school. At least this time I feel like if something does come up, there are better people in administration to handle it."

"Oh, yeah. Well, that's good. Uhm, Tangie?"

I closed the dishwasher and looked at my friend. "What's wrong?"

Beulah leaned against the counter, and threw the dish towel in her hand across her shoulder. "What's with *that* smile?"

I frowned, "What smile?"

She pointed at me, "The smile that just showed up on your face. I haven't seen one of those in a while. What or rather should I say who is on your mind?"

And just like that, Nathan Chambers appeared in my head again.

Why did thoughts of that man affect me like this?

Beulah clapped her hands together. "Spill it. Who is he?"

I walked closer to Beulah with my finger to my lips. "Shhhh, I don't need the boys to hear this."

Beulah swatted at me. "They have their head in that video game. Come outside, we can talk on the patio."

After a deep sigh, I followed her. I really didn't need to be spilling my sudden crush on Beulah. Then I thought maybe she could talk some sense into me. I mean this was a man at my son's school. He should totally be off limits.

Especially from my thoughts!

Seated outside under the gazebo, I told Beulah about my visit and how the school counselor had invaded my thoughts. "I don't know what happened to me."

"A man happened." Beulah Samuels exclaimed and then cackled.

I rolled my eyes. "I thought you were going to help me. I can't be doing this, Beulah."

She eyed me, "What exactly have you done? So, you're interested in an attractive man. You're a young woman. And you've been alone a long time, Tangie. I remember when you first came to the salon, girl you had your eye on any man that walked through the door. Then, you suddenly didn't seem to care anymore."

"That's because I didn't. I had young boys and I decided they needed to be my focus instead of wasting my time on knuckleheads."

I recalled my last conversations with Mama before she passed. *"Girl, you can be happy again. You're still so young. Life isn't over and your life is more than your boys. Don't do what I did. After your father left, I let go. I gave up on love."*

I looked over at Beulah. "I gave up. That woman you saw when I first worked at the salon was desperate for someone to take care of me, us. Then it hit me. God had sent me the man I thought I would spend the rest of my life with. Then God took him away." Tears flooded my eyes.

Beulah leaned over and patted my hand. "Oh honey, you were still grieving and lonely. You needed to give yourself more time."

I nodded, "No one else compared to him."

Drake's father was different from the twins' father. I met him when the twins were five and I was twenty-two. If life had turned out differently, Christan Nelson and I would still be together now. Ten years older than me, he was a good man who'd accepted me and my young twin boys, who had been conceived my senior year of high school. The twins, despite the absence of their biological father, took to Christan like he was their dad. We got married and Christan officially adopted Martin and Mark. Not too long after our first anniversary, we had Drake.

We had a home in the suburbs of Atlanta and I worked as a sales clerk at a J.C. Penney. On the weekend, I still did hair, tons of braids and weaves inside the basement of our home. Owning my own salon had been on the bucket list. Christan determined my dream would happen. He helped me heal from the wounds that held me bitter for so long after dealing with years of foolishness from the twins' dad.

Two years old, Drake was in the car with Christan that day. God was merciful, still using a car seat, Drake came away with a few bruises and scratches. The emergency personnel had to rip the car door off to get them out of the flipped car. Christan stayed in the hospital for eight days, but he never woke up. I moved back to my hometown Charlotte to be closer to Mama so she could help with the boys. It took me awhile to get myself together, to move past the grief. I went from one job to another until I ended up at Crown of Beauty.

The first few years working at the salon, I did try to get back out there with my mother and sisters' encouragement. I know my behavior seemed crazy to Candace and Beulah. Most of the time it felt crazy to me. There was no replacing Christan. Ever.

I gave up. My time came and was violently ripped from me.

For the longest, I kept it all inside hiding my pain behind my sharp witty personality. But losing Mama brought up the previous loss of my husband, and the loneliness enveloped me so fierce it scared me. I shared Christan's death with Candace and Beulah when I broke down over Mama's death. It was then I began going to Victory Gospel Church.

Beulah quietly spoke, "Your boys are getting older. They will be men soon. Who knows, maybe God is trying to tell you something?"

I scrunched my nose. "I'm pretty sure some of my thoughts aren't very Christian."

Beulah cackled again. "I'm trying to say to keep an open mind. God could place the right somebody in your path when you least expect it. Look at Candace and Darnell. Candace lost her first husband and she despaired for a while. She certainly wasn't expecting to meet Darnell. They will be celebrating seven years of marriage soon."

I thought about what Beulah said about our mutual friend Candace. I loved that about Candace and her second husband. They both showed the possibilities of love finding you again even after devastating loss.

Love found me once. I wasn't sure if I wanted to find it again. I needed to put Nathan Chambers out of my mind. That would be the best thing for me to do.

Chapter Four

The first few months of school flew by. By the time the first nine weeks ended, I hadn't thought much about Nathan Chambers. I didn't have time. Martin needed to get ready for basketball season. Mark always had something going on with band, either a Friday night football game or band competitions, and Drake had settled into The Lab and was an active part of the robotics team. There were days I didn't know which way was up. When I wasn't working at the salon, I was trying to make sure each of my sons had my support.

This sister was tired!

But thank the Lord, all my sons were in a good place. That's all that mattered to me. And, soon I would be able to step out on faith and invest in a second car.

Tonight, after missing two previous meetings, I finally made it to the PTO meeting at Drake's school. When I stepped in the cafeteria, I was fairly surprised to see the number of parents in attendance. A crowd mingled around two long tables, one held two large coffee carafes and the other, rows of food platters. Some platters appeared to be filled with veggies while others were definitely for someone with a sweeter palate. I headed towards the coffee. I'd been on my feet most of the day at the salon and needed the caffeine boost.

As I poured a cup of coffee, I side-eyed two women, one a platinum blond with a pixie cut and the other with deep auburn hair that fell in waves down her shoulder. I knew they had to be parents, but they stood together talking like two young girls.

"Girl, he is a dream. Did you notice he didn't have a ring on his finger?"

"Believe me I noticed. I wonder if he remembers me. You know I went to school with him. He was a big basketball star back then. I feel bad about his short time in the NBA, but yay for us, we get to see him around here."

Without even turning around, I guessed who the two women were talking about. Suddenly, my hands didn't feel that steady. I sat the cup of hot steaming coffee on the table and reached for two packets of sugar.

You need to play this cool, Tangie!

I gripped my coffee cup and turned around to search for a seat. When I was firmly in a chair at the end of a row, I scanned the room. My eyes fell on whom I sought. Nathan stood in the corner with the principal. I hadn't talked to Nathan in person since our meeting in his office. I glimpsed him a few times in the parking lot when I dropped off or picked Drake up from school. Our eyes always managed to connect even with a crowd of students around him. He would wave and I'd wave back. Even in those short moments of connection, I felt like some schoolgirl excited to see her crush pay attention to her.

During my quiet times, usually at night, I occasionally saw his photo in my Instagram feed. I wasn't looking for him, at least that's what I told myself. I liked to check up on what my boys were posting on Instagram. That was the main social media I followed them on. I didn't bother with Snapchat or TikTok. There was only so much foolishness I wanted to expose myself to at the end of my day.

When I did come across Nathan's Instagram posts, they were usually him at school with students or in the afterschool program where he mentored boys. That's how I found out he coached basketball at the Victory Gospel Church activity center. Funny how small the world could be. We attended the same church. *Who knew!* I'd never noticed Nathan at church before. Now that I knew, despite the mega-membership, his height made him stand out in the crowd. I also noted how people milled around him after services, but I never ventured to talk to him.

The two women I overheard chattering about Nathan interrupted my thoughts by plopping down in seats in front of me. For some reason, their chit-chat set my nerves on alert. My goal was to get away from them and here they were in my orbit again. Nathan was a good-looking man, but there was no need to stop acting like an adult. I did my best to block their conversation by catching up on emails. I became so engrossed in my phone I missed the start of the meeting.

After the meeting adjourned I talked to some parents, even the two women that sat in front of me. I found out they both had children in Drake's class that were also on the robotics team. I was pretty pleased with the changes in Drake, and coming to the meeting confirmed that The Lab was the perfect learning environment for him. Now I felt even better.

On my way out, I heard my name.

"Ms. Nelson?"

I turned to find Nathan walking towards me. I had this crazy thought of running for the exit, but I steeled myself, hoping the smile on my face didn't betray the turmoil going on inside. "Mr. Chambers, it's good to see you.

He smiled, but then his face went somber, "I wanted to talk to you about something that came up the other day. Drake talked to me about his dad."

What? I noticed we were blocking the entrance so I moved over to the side. Nathan followed me. I peered up at him, a bit overwhelmed by his statement. "Drake talked to you about his dad?"

He crossed his arms. "Yes, we have a father and son event that takes place in a few weeks. Something our principal started a few years ago. It's his way of getting more fathers involved." Nathan looked behind us, his grin wide. "As you can see, the parents who attend PTO lean heavily towards moms."

I peered around the cafeteria, which was starting to empty and nodded, "Sounds like a good idea. I can see how that could affect students whose dads are not in their life."

Nathan nodded, "Yes, Drake and I met a few times to check-in on how he's adjusting. I mentioned the event to him and that's when he told me his dad died when he was younger. I talked about my dad and how much I missed him. He passed away when I was in college. I know that's way different from Drake's experience."

"Oh, I'm sorry about your dad. Yeah, Drake was so young when he lost his dad. He doesn't talk or ask about him much now." I stuttered, "I really don't know how much he remembers him."

I wasn't sure why I was having this conversation with this man. I didn't talk to many people about Christan, only a few people, Mama, when she was alive, my sisters, Candace and Beulah.

"Well, is Drake doing okay? The only male figures he has in his life are my friends' husbands and at church. The youth pastor at Victory Gospel checks in on my boys from time to time."

Nathan smiled, "I believe Drake is a well-adjusted boy if that's what's worrying you. But, it doesn't hurt for him to talk to a male figure."

"Of course. I'm glad he can talk to you."

If I was being honest, I didn't encourage any talking about Christan. I kept his photos in the living room, my favorite being the one we took the day we all went to Six Flags Over Georgia. That was a fun day and a cherished memory. I'd packed the wedding photos into a box that sat at the top of my closet. The wedding ring was in my jewelry box.

Some memories were unbearable.

I suddenly felt warmth on my arm and looked down to find Nathan had touched my arm. I peered up at him, my mind jolted from my brief step back in time to the present.

Nathan snatched his hand away and crossed his arms. "Are you okay?"

"Yes." I smiled weakly, embarrassed. "Sorry, long day. I will talk to Drake, make sure to answer any questions he has about his dad. We don't talk enough and that's my fault. Maybe I can find someone from church to attend the upcoming event with him." I was babbling. *Why did I do that around this man?* Just spilling out my guts to him like he was my therapist or something.

I cleared my throat, "Was there something else you wanted to ask me?" Surely it wasn't to have this unexpected conversation about Drake's dad.

Or was he trying to get my attention for another reason.

I was still conscious of where his hand had been on my arm. I looked around the room to see if anyone else had noticed his touch, but the cafeteria had cleared out. The principal stood in a far corner talking to a pair that appeared to be parents. I turned my attention back to Nathan who had been watching me, his brown eyes intense. I may not have given Nathan Chambers much thought over the past few weeks, but I was reminded of the electrifying way the man opened up something in me the first time I saw him.

That didn't even happen with Christan. It took Christan a few times to get my attention. I was so hesitant to go out with him because he was older than me. But still, I took that chance.

I noticed Nathan nervously glance around as if he had to remind himself why we were talking together close to the school cafeteria exit. Clearing his throat, he responded to my question, "Oh yeah. I wanted to check to see if Drake brought you his progress report. We haven't received your signed copy back yet."

My heart dropped with something that felt like disappointment. *What else was I expecting him to say?*

"Yes, he did show it to me. I was very happy with how well he's doing." I frowned, "I'm sure

I signed it, but you know all my boys have so much going on right now, I could be thinking about something I signed for Martin or Mark. I can certainly check with Drake when I get home."

I dug in my purse for my car keys. Somehow I needed to break away from this awkward conversation.

Nathan grinned. "No problem! I can imagine this is a busy time of year for you. Can I walk you to your car?"

That shook me up. I gulped, "Uhm, sure."

Here I was trying to get away!

Normally I would have strode across the parking lot to my van, but I purposely let my long legs glide at a much slower pace. In a manner of a few minutes I'd experienced highs and lows that were making me feel almost giddy. My mouth didn't bother to slow down though, I started babbling as we walked, "My boys keep me jumping. But I'm happy they all have something to focus on. Keeps them out of trouble which is so important to me."

Nathan nodded, "That's good. It helps that the boys have activities to keep them disciplined."

Before I knew it we were standing beside my van.

Nathan turned, "So, you think South Meck High could be heading to the Division 4A Championship game again this year?"

I beamed, "Yes, if they can keep up the wins. I love that the championship games are at the Spectrum Center. That's exciting for high school players to be able to play where NBA teams play all the time. Martin was thrilled about playing in the arena last year."

Nathan returned my smile, "It's definitely an extraordinary experience for a young basketball player. Believe me, if the team keeps up this winning streak, I imagine you will be at the Spectrum Center to cheer from the stands."

"I would love it. I try to support my boys where I can." I clicked the key fob to open the doors. I simply couldn't stay outside talking with this man any longer, I was enjoying the conversation a bit too much.

Nathan reached over and pulled the driver's door open.

"Thank you," I said as I climbed into the van.

"You take care of yourself, Tangie."

Tangie. It was the first time in tonight's conversation he called my name.

"You too, Mr. ...Nathan. Have a blessed evening."

He closed the door and began to step away, backwards, his eyes focused on me.

I started the engine and then waved. He nodded in affirmation before turning around. I gripped the steering wheel, observing Nathan as he walked back inside the school. It wasn't until then I'd noticed how cool the interior of the van had become. The entire time I stood outside talking to Nathan, the autumn air didn't seem to affect me. Now I shivered. I had a feeling it was more than the chilly air affecting me.

I adjusted the heat setting to low, wondering again why my son's school counselor had such an effect on me.

Was Nathan feeling the same way I was feeling? Why did I care?

Before pulling out of the parking lot I looked over. A woman drove up in a white Mercedes in front of the school. Something told me to watch for a minute. My heart sank as I watched Nathan walk out of the school doors and climb into the car with the woman.

He was with someone already!

Well, that made sense. No way would a man like that be single. Still I felt like he was purposely trying to get my attention.

I sighed as the disappointment caused heat to rush into my cheeks, tears stung my eyes. How embarrassing, for the second time I just about made a fool of myself over this man.

I can't be that lonely.

Chapter Five

Life didn't slow down much. The holidays came and went. Despite glimpsing Nathan only on a few occasions, thoughts of him lingered, mainly wondering about the mysterious woman in his life. He must be a really private person because I never saw him with that woman or any woman on social media.

I had a weird desire to invite him over for the holidays, but fought it off. Then I fussed at myself for being cowardly.

After the new year, I berated myself and decided to face the facts. Nathan was a school counselor at my son's school. Surely that was a conflict of interest. I talked myself into the fact that I didn't have time for a relationship and my life revolved around my boys, making sure their hopes and dreams were fulfilled.

The talks I gave myself were not helping. In fact, for the first time in a long time, I was feeling off. Like life was moving past me and I was missing something.

One Wednesday in January, we'd officially closed the salon for the day. Candace found me sulking on the couch we kept behind the desk in the office. My head was in my hands, which wasn't a good look. She rushed over and touched my shoulders, "Hey, Tangie, is everything okay? Nothing is wrong with the boys, right?"

I lifted my head from my hands. "Yes, everything is fine. Sorry, I..."

How did I start this conversation? Everything wasn't really fine.

Candace sat beside me on the couch. "Something has been going on with you for a while. It started before the holidays. I've been waiting for you to come to me because I didn't want to pry. I thought maybe you were experiencing the loss of people in your lives. You know despite being married to Darnell, the past still gets to me especially during the holidays."

I shook my head, "During Thanksgiving and Christmas, I thought about Mama and Christan, but really it's not as bad as it used to be."

Candace smiled, "That's good. God is a healer." She looked away with some discomfort, "I did talk to Beulah over the holidays. She asked me something that surprised me."

I turned to face Candace. Every time I saw or talked to Beulah she always asked about Nathan, making me regret I ever confessed to her. I answered her the same. Nothing was happening because it wasn't meant to happen.

Candace continued, "She mentioned something about a man." She looked at me, her right eyebrow lifted with questions. "You've never mentioned this to me and I see you almost every day."

I threw my hands up as if defeated. "There's nothing to mention. He's the counselor at Drake's school. It would be totally inappropriate for us to consider a relationship. Besides I saw him with a woman one night, he's probably involved with someone."

Candace crossed her arms. "Well, you don't really have any control over when someone catches your attention. Has this guy made a move? Are you sure he has someone in his life?"

I frowned, "The few times we've met it seemed like he was interested. But I also saw him get into a car with a woman after a PTO meeting last fall. So his interest could've been my imagination because I had such a crazy reaction to him."

Candace grinned, waving her hands around, "You felt all girly around him. Butterflies in your stomach. Like he's the one."

We laughed.

Quietly, I said, "I didn't feel that way about either of my sons' dads. It took time for me to consider even going out with them. The twins' dad was your typical high school bad boy. Christan was the opposite, he was older, more mature." I sighed deeply, "The past few years I've been so used to going about my business, being alone didn't faze me. At least it hadn't until lately."

Candace rubbed her hands down her arms. "Well, you know when Darnell and I met, it was about as inappropriate as you can get. He was the lead detective in my best friend's murder. The times we had contact with each other should not have happened. He was investigating, and well I was sticking my nose in places I had no business. But I knew he was on my side and I also felt like there was something there. That something that you think you can only feel once in a lifetime with someone. Is that how you're feeling?"

"I guess." I smacked my hand to my forehead, "I don't know, Candace. What I do know is I can't stop crushing on this guy. I'm too old for this."

Candace laughed, "You are not! There is some reason why." She looked at me thoughtfully for a moment, "I also wasn't sure how my kids were going to react to me moving on with someone who wasn't their dad. Frank's death was still pretty raw for all of us. You haven't dated much in years. How do the boys feel?"

I swallowed, "You know Martin asked me a while ago, why didn't I date. I thought that was the weirdest question coming from him. Drake was so young when he lost his dad. He talked to Nathan about his dad, which is strange. He never asks me or at least he hasn't since he was little."

"Nathan. Is that this counselor's name?" Candace smiled. "First name basis, huh?"

I shook my head. "Nathan Chambers. He actually was a big basketball star in his heyday. Made it all the way to the NBA." I rolled my eyes at Candace's questioning gaze, "Yes, before you ask me how I knew that, I googled him." I cringed, "I even follow him on Instagram."

Candace chuckled, "Girl, that's what you have to do these days. I say it shows you're seriously interested."

I stood and paced the small office. "I don't know. I don't want to be chasing him."

Candace sat back on the couch. "You think he should make the first move? I agree. So what are you going to do in the meantime? You can't be walking around all melancholy."

I crossed my arms, "I am not doing that."

"You know when Beulah retired, we discussed how much energy you bring to the salon. It's why she passed on the co-ownership to you. We agreed your passion and ideas were what Crown of Beauty needed. Life is good for you now compared to last school year. You were living a parent's nightmare. All that has been resolved. But you're still not back to yourself, Tangie. As nutty as Beulah can be, I have to agree with her. Maybe you need to remain open to the possibility. Suppose Nathan can sense your hesitation?"

I held up my hands, "Well, what am I supposed to do?"

Before Candace could respond, my phone rang. I looked down at the screen and noticed Drake's photo. I answered the phone. "Drake, what's going on?" I glanced at my watch, "You're at the house, right?"

"No, Mom. I missed the bus."

Panic clutched me, "What? Why didn't you call me before now? You've been at the school all this time."

"Yeah, but it's fine. Mr. Chambers can bring me home, but he wanted me to call you to make sure that's okay."

"Mr. Chambers is with you?" I glanced over at Candace who stared back with concern. "Look, I'm getting ready to leave the salon, but it will take me at least thirty minutes to get to you in this traffic. Martin and Mark should be home. If Mr. Chambers doesn't mind dropping you off at the house, tell him I appreciate it."

"Cool, see you at home, Mom."

I looked down at my phone.

"What's going on?" Candace asked. "Did you say Mr. Chambers?"

I nodded, "He's taking Drake home. That boy missed the bus. He never does that."

"Well, sounds like you better get going. I have a feeling something is about to change for you." Candace winked at me.

My stomach flip-flopped. Nathan was headed to my house. Maybe he would just drop Drake off and keep going. I hoped so because at the moment I was freaking out on how much I'd been keeping up with my housekeeping. Knowing my schedule, not very well. With a hasty goodbye to Candace, I grabbed my bag and flew through the salon out to my car.

Chapter Six

Forty minutes later, I turned into my driveway and noticed an Audi SQ5 in front of my home. I'd never seen the vehicle before and assumed Mr. Chambers was still here. I groaned my despair, feeling as if a heat wave had taken over my body despite the cool air blasting through the car vents.

Nathan Chambers is in my house.

This was a development I could have never prepared for and now was not the time to be freaking out. I didn't need my boys witnessing their mom have a meltdown.

So, I pulled myself together and exited the van. Despite my best effort to display confidence, my legs felt like they were disconnected from my body as I climbed the stairs to my front porch.

I kept a huge amount of keys on my keychain, most I didn't even know what they opened. For some reason today, of all days, I couldn't locate the house key. I berated myself for the hundredth time thinking why didn't I get those plastic things to identify keys.

My front door suddenly swung open causing me to drop my pile of keys to the ground.

My youngest son grinned at me. "Mom, Mr. Chambers is still here. We ordered pizza."

I frowned, "What?" Before I could get an answer to my question, Drake took off down the hallway leaving me standing in the doorway stunned. Not only was Nathan Chambers in my house, but he's eating pizza. I reached down for my keys and stepped inside, my emotions were all over the place now. I couldn't tell if I was nervous about Nathan being here or if it was a surge of anger that he'd seemed to have invited himself to stay. I placed my bag and keys on the foyer table and squared my shoulders.

Let's do this, girl!

My march down the hall towards the kitchen slowed as I heard voices. I recognized Martin's voice, "Man, that three pointer you took against North Meck during the championship was awesome. Coach Winters still brags on that shot to us."

Nathan's voice answered, "Seriously? Believe me that was pure luck. The clock was counting down and you know, you just gotta take that chance."

I stepped inside the kitchen as the conversation kicked up a notch with Drake and Mark both jumping in. I found myself transfixed by the picture before me. My three boys were sitting around the dining room table with Nathan in the middle. Some days it was a struggle to get all of us to sit at the table together, and it had been years since there was an adult male at my table.

My eyes met Nathan's across the room. His eyes were warm as a smile spread across his face.

Suddenly feeling shy, I looked away and concentrated on fixing my gaze on Drake. "So, someone missed the school bus today?"

Drake protested. "But I didn't mean to. We were working on the robot for the competition next week."

Nathan pushed the chair back from the table, "Ms. Nelson, that was probably my fault. The team was hard at work on some glitches and time slipped by." Standing to his full height, "I realize I probably stayed longer than I should have. Let me get out of the way so you and your boys can enjoy dinner."

Martin frowned at Nathan, "You're staying, right?" He swiveled his attention to me. "Mom, let him stay. We were talking and the pizza will be here soon."

I couldn't help it, I huffed. "Who decided to order pizza again? There's food in the freezer you could have unthawed."

The doorbell rang.

Drake yelled, "It's here." I turned and watched as my son ran past me. Then, I lifted my hands in defeat. "You may as well stay for dinner, Mr. Chambers." I walked over to the cabinet to pull out the paper plates I kept on hand.

He grinned, "Thank you, and it's Nathan. Can I help?"

I turned, startled to see Nathan standing behind me. *He moved fast.*

"Uh, no, you're a guest. And thank you, Nathan, for bringing Drake home. I know that had to have taken you out of your way."

"It wasn't a problem. I actually don't live far from here."

"Oh." For some reason his statement made my face feel flush again. I turned and opened the fridge, needing to focus my attention anywhere but Nathan's face. "What can I offer you to drink? We have ice tea, lemonade, ginger ale and bottled water."

"Bottled water will be fine."

I reached for the bottle and handed it to him. Nathan's long fingers brushed against my hand. My eyes locked with his for a few seconds. The moment was broken by the voices of my sons in the background tearing into the pizza boxes now on the counter.

"Hey, guys, where are your manners? Use the plates." I rolled my eyes and turned my attention to Nathan. "You would think I didn't feed them."

He laughed, "They're growing boys."

The next thirty minutes, I smiled and laughed at my boys as they sparred over pizza slices and traded conversation with Nathan. He appeared to be right at home. My nervousness from earlier dissipated, instead replaced by comfort. It felt like Nathan had always been at our table.

Before I knew it, the boys had left the kitchen and I was alone. Nathan took it upon himself to crush the pizza boxes and place them in the garbage cans outside.

After he entered back through the side door, he headed over to the sink to wash his hands. I finished wiping down the island with a dish cloth. "You know my boys should have done that."

"It's the least I could do." He reached over and grabbed a paper towel to dry his hands. "I want to thank you for your hospitality. I had a good time tonight with you and your boys."

"I did too." Feeling a bit tired, I put the dish cloth down and pulled out a stool to sit. "Thank you for looking out for Drake. I appreciate it."

Nathan tossed the paper towel in the trash and then sat on one of the island's stools on the side where I'd just sat. "You're doing a great job with your sons. You should be proud of all of them."

I nodded, feeling very aware of Nathan's presence near me. "I am proud of them."

He cleared his throat. "You should know about another conversation I had with Drake."

I sat up straight. "What's wrong?" I cocked my ear to listen at the kitchen door expecting Drake or one of my other sons to appear. "Did he mention his dad again?"

Nathan shook his head. "No, his concern was for his mom."

"Me?" I touched my chest, alarm bells were going off in my head. "What did he say?"

Appearing amused by my panic, Nathan clasped his hands together before explaining, "He's concerned that you spend all your time working for him and his brothers. That you don't know how to have fun."

My shoulders dropped as I let out a breath. "What? I do know how to have fun, I just ... I don't have time."

He wrinkled an eyebrow. "Sounds like Drake was on to something."

I folded my arms and eyed him. "Why would this interest you? And haven't we held you up long enough tonight? You have to have someone at home waiting on you."

Nathan peered down at his watch. "Just my dog. I'm sure he's upset about not being fed yet."

"A dog? That's all. Surely, you have someone."

He grinned, "Are you asking if I'm dating anyone?"

My face flushed with embarrassment, I retorted, "No, that's not what I asked."

"But you are wondering if I have someone at home waiting, like a girlfriend?"

I couldn't help but look down at his hand. "It doesn't appear you are married."

"You noticed."

I smiled. "Yes, I don't need some woman coming after me."

"Well, you don't have to worry about that."

So, he claimed he wasn't with anyone but still I remembered the PTO meeting last fall. How could I inquire about the woman who picked him up without showing that I'd clearly been interested for a while. Then it came to me.

Why not let him know?

This entire evening was not perchance, and I had a sneaky feeling that my boys just didn't accept Nathan Chambers in our house this evening out of the blue, even if he was a former NBA basketball player.

I decided to plunge forward. "You remember the PTO meeting last fall when you walked me to my van?"

Nathan nodded, "I remember. I wanted to talk to you."

I smirked, "I got the impression you wanted my attention more than about Drake."

"I did, but something told me to back off. You seemed like you weren't ready."

"Probably for a good reason, a woman came to pick you up."

He stared at me, "You saw that!" Then he laughed, "Wait, you didn't think? That woman was my sister. My car was in the shop and she picked me up."

I responded weakly, "Your sister?"

"Yes." He leaned forward, "I know I'm Drake's guidance counselor, but I knew the moment I met you that I wanted to get to know you. You are a smart, beautiful business woman. A single mom raising three brilliant young men. When I walked across the room that night it was my intention to ask you out for coffee, but something told me it wasn't the right time."

I gulped, trying to process Nathan's words to me. "So, how do you feel now after spending the evening in my home with my boys?"

He reached over and took my hand in his. "If you're interested, I'd like to officially ask you out on a date."

I took a deep breath. "I would love to go on date with you."

"Saturday night? I'll pick you up at six o'clock."

"It's a date."

I felt that disconnect from my body again as I walked Nathan to the door. Long after I closed the door, I stood wondering about the entire evening. *Was this a dream?*

"Mom, are you okay?"

I turned around and saw Drake on the stairs watching me.

"Yes, it's been a long day. Shouldn't you be in the bed by now?"

"I heard Mr. Chambers leave."

"Yes," I eyed him. "And what are you doing telling people I don't know how to have fun?"

He shrugged. "He's always asking about you. You do the same thing."

I stared at him. "Wait, he asks you about me?"

"Yeah, he's like 'how's your mom doing?'" Drake rolled his eyes. "And you are always asking, 'have you seen Mr. Chambers today?' I figured you two just needed to talk to each other."

My mouth fell open. Had I been that obvious to my own son? "So, you decided to do some matchmaking?"

He grinned, "Looks like it worked."

Then he ran back up the stairs leaving me speechless.

Chapter Seven

The next day before I could set up for my first client at the salon, Candace wanted to know everything. By the time I spilled all the events of the night before, she was jumping up and down like a schoolgirl.

"What, what, are you kidding me? And Drake set that up?"

I shrugged. "Apparently, I'm not as good at hiding my feelings as I thought. Anyway, I have my first date in years on Saturday and I hope that I'm still functional by then."

Candace clasped her hands together. "I'm so happy for you." She grabbed my shoulders. "This is your time. It's time for you to be happy. Everyone wants this for you. Even your sons."

Tears sprang to my eyes. "I'm trying not to trip, but it was wonderful how Nathan got along with the boys. You know that's the scary thing and one of the reasons I just stopped dating. My boys are everything to me and we come as a package deal."

Package deal. Despite it being Saturday, all of my sons were home. Most Saturdays they were out with friends. Not tonight. When the doorbell rang, one of the twins answered the door. I wasn't too bothered since I wasn't quite ready yet. I could hear Nathan conversating downstairs as I applied my lipstick. I took one last look in the full length mirror in my room. The pile of clothes that I'd rejected for tonight's date lay on my bed. Nathan didn't mention where we were going, so I came up with a bright fuchsia blouse that appeared dressy but could convert to casual pretty quickly since I'd worn my black jeans over black ankle boots.

When I appeared at the living room door where Nathan sat, he and my boys turned around to stare at me. "Well, I hope I don't look like an alien."

"You look great, Mom." "Nice." Comments and smiles from my boys warmed my heart.

Nathan approached me holding a bouquet of roses in his hands. "You look beautiful. These are for you."

I smiled. "Thank you, Nathan. Let me put these in water."

Drake jumped up from the couch. "I can do that for you, Mom."

Surprised by his offer, I stuttered. "O-Okay, Drake. Thank you."

Next thing I knew, Nathan was holding open his car door for me. Once inside, I nervously glanced back at the house. Nathan climbed inside the driver's seat. He laughed, "Your boys are quite protective of their mom. I don't remember getting the third degree like that since taking a girl out for prom."

I whipped my head around, "No, they didn't? I'm so sorry."

He winked. "Don't! You're raising gentlemen and they wanted to be sure my intentions were on the up and up with their mom."

My body was warm all the way down to my toes and it had nothing to do with the toasty heat from inside the car.

Nathan drove into downtown Charlotte to South Caldwell street. "Have you ever been to Fahrenheit Restaurant?"

I shook my head, "I've never been here before."

A valet stepped up to our car.

"Good, I wanted this to be a unique experience. You're going to love Chef Rocco Whalen."

We rode the elevator to the twenty-first floor. The host clearly recognized Nathan, and we were seated a few minutes after arriving. The combination of the dining room's intimate atmosphere, and the view of Charlotte's city skyline was stunning.

"This is beautiful, Nathan. You certainly don't play around on the first date."

"I wanted to take you somewhere special. This is one of my favorite views in the city."

Nathan ordered the Cowboy Ribeye entree, while I opted for the Soy-Glazed Salmon. Despite our elegant surroundings, I felt comfortable talking to Nathan, sharing some recent adventures with my sons as well as some stories from the salon.

The waiter cleared our dinner plates. "I feel like I've been doing most of the talking."

Nathan wiped his mouth with his cloth napkin. "I've enjoyed listening to you. You are a remarkable woman. Really it wasn't until I decided to go into teaching and started working with students that I can say my life served a purpose. Don't get me wrong, I enjoyed playing ball, it came with its perks but also some vices."

"None of us have a perfect life, Nathan. I'm definitely not one to talk. I had my twins really young and it's been a struggle."

Nathan looked at me, "You're amazing. I can tell you've been through a lot, but you're a strong woman."

"Only as strong as I can be with God on my side. My boys are growing up, becoming men. It's a scary time in the world and I depend a lot on prayer. I have good folks in my circle."

Nathan examined me across the table, "I hope I can be a part of that circle."

I smiled, "I would like that."

The drive back to my house was quiet, but not uncomfortable. As Nathan pulled into the driveway, I noted the house was dark with a few flickers of light from the boys' bedrooms upstairs. I was pretty sure those lights were reflections from some serious video gaming.

I wasn't quite ready to leave the warmth of Nathan's vehicle and turned to face him.

He let the engine run, sensing I may not be ready to exit the car. The January temperatures had dropped considerably since the beginning of our evening. He commented, "I had a good time this evening."

"I did too."

"So, can we plan to do this again soon?"

I smiled, "Planning for the second date already? I would love to see what you come up with next. Going to be hard to top that."

He laughed, "I will work out something, but you know what I would love more?"

I peered over at him, "Tell me."

"If this could be forever one day. I know we have a lot to learn about each other, but I want you to know this is serious for me. Spending time with you. Getting to know your boys. It's a privilege and I'm grateful to God for the opportunity."

I swallowed. "You are something else, Nathan Chambers. I can't deny that I want to see where this goes too."

He leaned in, "I'm glad we're on one accord."

I leaned forward. When our lips touched, I knew love had indeed found me.

Holding On To Love

A Novella

"Trust in the Lord with all your heart, and do not lean on your own understanding. In all your ways acknowledge him, and he will make straight your paths." Proverbs 3:5-6

Chapter One

I couldn't wipe the grin off my face if I tried. Someone might have thought I'd won the lottery, but most people in Crown of Beauty Salon already knew about my blessings. My story had become well-known in the community. I was a single mother of three boys, and my twins were graduating in a few months. One of those twins, Martin Nelson, made his own mark in the world recently helping his team win the state championship as point guard on South Meck's high school basketball team. So, most people knew me as the mom yelling and cheering for my son.

In the past year, I had a companion by my side also cheering Martin on. Former NBA player, Nathan Chambers. I'd found love for the second time in my life, or rather love found me. I definitely wasn't looking for it. It had been me and my boys until Nathan.

My fiancé.

I noticed I'd been absently twisting the engagement ring on my finger and stopped. Instead, I clasped my hands together in front of me. I had plenty of stylists booked in the salon today. So on days when I wasn't doing hair, I kept the ring on my finger. As a precaution, if I had to have my hand in soapy water to wash a client's hair, I kept the ring tucked away in my bag in the salon's office.

I never expected to be engaged to be married again. My first husband had succumbed to injuries in a car crash eight years ago. All these years later, I'd settled into single motherhood. But the man I was intensely watching on the television screen had captured my heart.

Usually bustling with chatter, the salon remained quiet today with only the sounds of flat irons clicking and splashes of water from the sink area. Everyone close to the salon's television, including me, watched as Nathan chatted on the WSIC Morning News Show. It could have been my imagination, but the morning host seemed enamored with Nathan. She smiled and tossed her blond highlighted hair a few times. I discovered that most women were flustered around Nathan. I couldn't say I was totally used to it, but Nathan always made me feel special, like I was the only one for him.

I'm not worried about any other woman. He is mine. I am his.

How was it possible that he looked even more handsome today? His chocolate skin almost glowed under the bright studio lights. He'd recently cut his hair low and shaved off the beard he'd been sporting since the fall. I wasn't a beard woman, but I'd grown to like the distinguished gentleman look. Nathan and I were the same age, thirty-four, but the gray streaks in his beard made him appear older.

Today, freshly-shaven, he reminded me of the first time I met him at the Charlotte STEM Lab, also known as "The Lab," where my youngest son attended school. Nathan's eyes were warm and radiated confidence as he chatted with the host. I watched his lips move.

Mmmm, lips I knew up close and personal.

The host asked, "Mr. Chambers, how have you been able to transition from playing in the NBA to being a guidance counselor?"

Nathan flashed his million-dollar smile. "I love it. One of the best career moves I could have made. Well, of course, the ankle injury helped me along, but I have no regrets. I help young people, who would be overlooked in other schools, be able to excel in math and science. And I really enjoy coaching the robotics team. In fact, if I hadn't been so caught up in playing basketball in school, I'm sure I would have been an engineer."

I laughed softly. My youngest son, Drake, was an incredibly bright boy who took after his deceased father. My brilliant child was known to enjoy reading the encyclopedia. Nathan and I both agreed that Drake would probably follow in his dad's footsteps and become an engineer. He had the aptitude for it and I was glad that he'd been given the opportunity to explore and excel.

It was crazy that over a year ago, while attending public school, Drake had gotten into a fight with a bully. This unfair attack led to Drake being suspended. But despite this small setback, God had a master plan with The Lab accepting Drake into their school program.

"You must be so proud."

Not recognizing the voice, I turned to find a beautiful woman with smooth honey-colored skin. I'd never seen her before, but something about her seemed oddly familiar. One of our newest hair stylist, Wanda, was flat ironing the woman's hair.

I smiled at the woman, trying to think where I'd seen her before and how would she know about my connection to Nathan. I twisted my engagement ring again. "Do I know you? Is this your first time here?"

The woman's hazel eyes appeared bright and shiny. I suspected they were contacts, but you could never be sure. Her eyes shifted down to my hands and then slowly back up to my face, like she was checking me out. "I'm new in Charlotte. I haven't been here long, but I saw you on Nathan's Instagram profile. You're his fiancée."

I felt the curve of my mouth slip downward. I received this kind of attention more than I cared for. There were some disadvantages to being in a relationship with a former NBA star. "Yes, I am. Thank you for choosing Crown of Beauty for your hair care needs today." I glanced at Wanda who was almost finished flat ironing the woman's hair.

The woman answered back. "I appreciate the service."

We locked eyes for a few seconds before I turned my attention back to the television. I hated that I'd missed part of the conversation. Suddenly, I felt self-conscience about turning my back. I could almost feel the woman's eyes boring into my back.

Who is she? Why is she giving me the creeps?

The anchorwoman was asking Nathan another question. "Tell us more about The Assist Group. What is it you hope to achieve?"

"Thank you for the question. The Assist Group is a foundation I started two years ago. I've been out of the game of basketball for about four years now, but I'm still in touch with my old colleagues. I have at least five NBA players who have pledged their support for the programs being offered through The Assist Group. Basically, we are here to support students, primarily middle grades. I kept thinking about when I was in school and the only real opportunities offered to me were sports. I would have loved to have been more exposed to opportunities in STEM."

The host interrupted. "Just for our viewers who may not be familiar, what is STEM?"

Nathan gave her a head nod. "Yeah, right. STEM stands for science, technology, engineering and mathematics. There are tons of opportunities to go into these high technology fields. The Assist Group has started with supporting programs here in Charlotte, like the robotics program at

The Lab. We sponsor the team making sure they have access to equipment and the ability to travel to competitions."

"Sounds so exciting. I understand you have friends in the NBA who have taken up the cause in their own cities?"

"That's correct. We're looking to branch into Florida next."

The host clasped her hands together. "I heard you used to be tight with Drex Armstrong. Could he be one of the players you are bringing on board?"

For a moment, Nathan's smile slipped, but he caught himself. "Yes, I'm in talks with Drex. He would be an amazing supporter of the program."

"Thank you, Mister Chambers. Our viewers will be excited to hear how you have moved past your injuries and found a passion for helping young people."

As the morning show went to a commercial, I frowned. The host didn't have to go there. It was true that at one time Nathan and Drex were tight as brothers, even playing for the same team. Nathan's injuries tore him away from his old friends. I also knew Drex had moved in on Nathan's woman at the time. Or rather his woman decided she preferred to stick with an NBA player as a mate.

I turned away from the television to catch a glimpse of Candace, my co-owner, as she headed back to the office. Almost ten years ago, Candace took a chance on me when I wasn't really in a good place. She hired me to be a stylist at the salon. I knew there were times back then when I worked her last nerve. But the Christian woman she is helped groom me into the woman I am today. She also saved me from making a horrible mistake.

I glanced back at Wanda's station and noticed the strange woman was no longer sitting at the booth. I looked at the front of the salon and didn't glimpse her at the cash register.

She must have left.

I don't know why, but there was something about her that bothered me. Most people were aware of my relationship with Nathan, but no one pointed out the fact that they'd seen me on his Instagram profile. Last time I checked Nathan's IG, it wasn't a lot of photos of us. I didn't take selfies that often, and when I was photographed it was usually with one or all my sons.

I tried to rack my brain for the last photo I'd taken with Nathan. It had to be last October. Someone snapped a picture of Nathan and I cheering in the stands at South Meck high school. It was March, and due to the frequency of Nathan's posts, that photo would be way down on his IG profile. Not wanting to give it anymore thought, I headed towards the office in the back of the salon.

Candace looked up from where she'd been opening a box of hair care supplies. I spied shampoo, conditioner and some curly cream from a natural hair representative who'd recently visited the shop. Both Candace and I liked the formula which was created by two black mothers. I'd been natural a long time choosing to wear my hair in braids, twists and on occasion, goddess locs. Candace had recently gone natural in the last year but liked blowing her hair out and wearing her classic bob she'd been sporting for years. Her hair had turned salt and pepper since I'd met her a decade ago, but she still looked the same.

Candace turned her monitor around showing the familiar Facebook interface. On the screen was a video player with a screenshot of Nathan's face. "Nathan did great. The camera loves him. I know you are so proud of him."

"I am proud of him. I didn't know the station streamed this on their Facebook page."

"Yes, you'll be able to watch it again and again."

I laughed. "I don't know if I will, but I'm sure Nathan is going to and gripe about how he did. He does really great work, but there are times he pushes himself a bit too hard. That last question the host asked was a bit invasive."

"Oh, you mean about Drex Armstrong? They played together, right?"

"Yes, but Nathan hasn't talked to Drex since his injuries, although it had more to do with women issues. Drex married Nathan's former fiancée."

"Ouch. I didn't realize that. I imagine that's a sore spot for Nathan."

I grinned. "It was until I came along."

Candace burst out laughing. "Of course. You put any woman he was ever with to shame. He only has eyes for you."

I laughed with Candace, feeling the spark of hope that washed over me when I thought about Nathan and our pending nuptials.

"So how are the wedding plans going? I know it was a bit impossible when Martin and Mark were traveling with South Meck High for basketball games."

I grimaced. "Yeah, things have slowed down with the twins, but graduation is around the corner. And both boys are waiting to hear back from the colleges they applied to. With so much going on, I want to keep this wedding simple."

Candace tilted her head. "You know you can reach out to Lenora Freeman to assist. This is her thing."

Lenora Freeman, the first lady of Victory Gospel Church, owned Lenora's Bridal Boutique. "I might have to. I reached out to her a while ago. She does have two wedding planners that work for her, but I wasn't sure I wanted to commit. I have the checklist she gave me, but it still seems like so much to do. I just know next I have to get my dress, the bridesmaids' dresses and we have to pick out a cake. Oh, yeah, and the counseling session with Reverend Freeman. I'm not sure how I feel about that. I didn't do all this the first time around when I got married. We just went to the justice of the peace."

"I know, but that's why you should go all out this time. It's a lot of work; but it's going to be your day, Tangie."

"You have always had my back with this engagement. Just to think I almost said no." Yeah, this wedding almost wasn't going to happen. I foolishly hesitated when Nathan popped the question, not understanding that God was giving me a second chance. This would be my second marriage and Nathan's first. He'd been a bachelor all these years. Sometimes it was too hard for me to grasp how he'd not been snatched up during his NBA career.

I looked over at the big clock on the wall. "Nathan's family is coming over for dinner tonight at his place. You know how that stresses me. I need to get out of here early and make sure my boys are ready. I will see you all on Monday at Lenora's Bridal Boutique."

Candace waved. "I wouldn't miss it! I love weddings, girl. And no problem on leaving early, Wanda and Jackie will close up. Just be sure to not let anyone get to you, okay. I know his family knows you are the best thing that ever happened to him."

He might be the best thing that happened to me. Really us.

Nathan had managed to make us a whole unit; something I hadn't realized I needed. Even more astonishing to me, Nathan had been accepted by my boys who experienced the same loss I did.

My twins, Martin and Mark never had a relationship with their father who skipped out as soon as he found out I was pregnant. At seventeen, to the disappointment of my mother, I'd followed in my older sister's footsteps and fallen into the cycle of teenage pregnancy in our family.

Years later, when the twins were five, I fell seriously in love with the man who would become my first husband.

Christian Nelson took the role of being a father to two young boys with joy. His death devastated the twins just as it did me. While Drake, my only child with Christian, was three years old, he had faint memories of his dad that he held with a tight fist. All of my boys had managed to find something in common with Nathan. For Martin, it was obviously basketball. For Drake, Nathan had a chance to embrace his nerdy side with my youngest. Mark was the family musician as well as South Meck's drum major. While his twin hit the court, Mark was in the stands leading the band. Surprisingly, both Nathan and Mark had a similar passion for jazz.

How could I not marry the man I'd fallen in love with and who'd embraced my sons? That was a single mother's hope and prayer in a relationship. I had to constantly remind myself to not get caught up in my feelings and fears. The dating life had not been good to me and the one man I loved was snatched away. I couldn't help but feel like my relationship with Nathan was too good to be true.

Trust in the Lord, Tangie.

Chapter Two

I didn't come from a large family and thankfully neither did Nathan. Growing up, I had my mother, who passed away almost six years ago, and two older sisters. And I considered Candace and our former salon owner, the now retired Beulah Samuels as my family. I also had ladies in my bible study who'd become like sisters to me. The women in my life were better to me than my own blood-related sisters. Both of my sisters lived in Atlanta and I only saw them a few times a year, but recently they had expressed more excitement about my upcoming marriage than I'd witnessed in years. I'm sure it had to do with bringing a former NBA player into the family.

I'm not so sure Nathan's family saw any benefit to him marrying a hairstylist with three sons. I tried to impress, which was why I was in Nathan's kitchen preparing food. I'd marinated the chicken breasts and now had them sizzling on top of the indoor grill. Nathan had a state-of-the-art kitchen that put my small kitchen to shame. His appliances included an oven with an air fryer, which I loved.

We'd already talked about us all moving into Nathan's five bedroom, three and half bath home. Each of the boys would have their own room which had been a tight squeeze at our house. With only three bedrooms, I gave the twins the master bedroom so they could have plenty of space. That left me with the bedroom between the twins and Drake. Often times I didn't get much peace in between video games, but I insisted everyone use headphones. Drake and I shared a bathroom which could be complicated because Drake moved slower than anyone else in the house. All of that would be behind us once we moved into Nathan's place.

Being over at Nathan on Fridays, and sometimes into the weekend, had become a thing. I shied away from it at first, but Nathan, an avid video gamer himself, loved the company. I'd grown up in a female dominant household, now as an adult, my household was filled with testosterone. At least at Nathan's there was space for me to enjoy girly stuff. I'd even dreamed about having a girl, but I kept that to myself. Drake was eleven years old, which meant it'd been that long since I had a baby.

"Tangie!" I quickly tried to straighten the grimace on my face when I heard Nathan's sister, Nadia Chambers-Lester. I always heard Nadia before I saw her. She had one of those voices that carried over several rooms. She wasn't yelling but projected her raspy voice, I believe out of habit.

Nadia had been an educator for almost twenty years. Despite Nathan veering off into athletics, his second career was an easy transition since he grew up with his mother and father being educators. Nathan lost his dad when he was a teenager, but there were plenty of photos of the former principal, both in Nathan's house and his mother's home.

Nadia stood in the kitchen archway with her hands on her hips. She was a full-figured woman who was, at five foot-nine, not as tall as her younger brother. Closer to my height, she didn't let her weight deter her love of clothes. Even now on a Friday evening, Nadia was dressed eloquently, wearing a gold tunic over burnt orange slacks.

I'd thought Nathan's mom would be the one to give me grief. Monica Chambers wasn't that warm to me, but she was always polite. I'd learned from being around Monica that she was just reserved. In fact, Nathan received a lot of his demeanor from his mother.

Nadia, on the other hand, was all about protecting her younger brother. She could come off sounding loud and obnoxious. From our first meeting it was obvious she didn't like that I came pre-packaged. She didn't outright disrespect my boys, but they all had indicated that her tone seemed overly harsh like she expected them to get into something.

I found this incredibly annoying since Nadia was in her own blended family. In fact, the woman was on her third marriage which included three children from her first husband and three children from two other husbands. Her current husband was a sweetheart. Nathan adored the women in his family and vice versa. Monica had raised him well and he knew how to treat a woman."

"Tangie, what is that?" Nadia barked as she drew closer to the counter. Most of the time I couldn't tell if she was scolding me or just speaking my name out loud.

"Hello, Nadia. I'm keeping it simple tonight since I had to work in the salon today. We're having grilled chicken and I started on a salad over there." I wasn't expecting Nadia to help. She never offered. Instead, she cracked opened the fridge and pulled out a bottle of red wine. Nathan didn't drink wine but kept it around for his sister.

"It smells good." Nadia glanced around Nathan's kitchen. "You sure are at home in this place."

I am about to marry your brother.

But that seemed to be something Nadia remained in denial about, which kind of disturbed me. It was like she thought me and the boys didn't belong in Nathan's home.

She walked over and peeked under a dish I'd wrapped in aluminum foil.

"I made peach cobbler last night. There's some vanilla ice cream. I know it's Nathan's favorite."

Nadia eyed me. "You are good in the kitchen. I will give that."

I decided not to take offense. I figured after Nathan and I were married, I would let Nadia know the real me. Which in most cases needed a helping of Jesus to keep my own mouth under control. I was thankful. Over the years, I'd learned the art of being calm. I was conscience of how much Nathan loved his older sister and didn't want to rock the boat. I didn't consider myself a whiner, so venting about how Nadia didn't like me very much was not an option.

I could feel Nadia's eyes on me as I placed the grilled chicken on a dish. I turned, not even caring if my annoyance showed on my face. I was tired and this woman wasn't helping. "Did you need something, Nadia?"

She shook her head. "Nope. Just came to see how things were going with you."

I really wished we could get past the awkwardness between us. Nadia lived here in Charlotte, but we rarely got together except when her brother decided he wanted a family night. I decided to attempt more of a conversation. "How are the kids and Steven doing?" I figured most people should be able to talk about their family. I know I could run my mouth about my boys anytime.

"They're doing fine. Steven didn't come with me this time."

That surprised me. Her husband was always by her side. Now granted, she bossed the man around, making everyone feel sorry for him. "Oh, I see. Is everything alright?" I cringed as soon as I said it. "I'm sorry, I'm not trying to pry. Steven always comes. Nathan and his brother-in-law seem like two peas in a pod."

Nadia smiled slightly. "Yes, they do get along. Nathan actually likes Steven, which was more than I can say for my first two husbands. Nathan likes to tease me that I should have paid more attention to him. Look, good talking to you. I'm going to see how Mama is doing."

"Yeah. Good talking." I sighed deeply, letting my tense shoulders relaxed.

At that moment Nathan entered. He passed his sister, who turned to look up at him. "Well, there you are. I've been looking for you."

"Hey, Sis. I didn't hear you come in."

"Mama let me in. You must be busy." Nadia glanced at me. "Came in here looking for you."

That explained some of the awkwardness. She came in here looking for her brother. The last person she wanted to see was me because then she would have to talk to me and acknowledge that I existed. I walked over to the fridge and grabbed the big bowl of salad. Drake and Mark did help me quickly assemble the salad earlier.

As Nathan and his sister chatted behind me, I kept myself busy. I was so focused; I didn't realize Nadia had left until Nathan sneaked up behind me. Strong arms came around my waist and pulled me close. Any remaining stress from my encounter with his sister melted away. I leaned back into the chest of the man who'd brought me such joy in the past year. Once his lips connected with my neck, I almost forgot I was in the kitchen.

"Nathan Chambers, you sure know how to distract a woman."

"You looked like you needed some attention. I appreciate you cooking for tonight, but we all could have gone out to eat, you know. You've been on your feet all day at the salon."

I turned and gazed up at brown eyes that were full of concern. "I'm fine. Besides, we have plenty of stylists working now. I spent most of the day getting supplies ordered and stocking the shelves. Candace knew how important it was for me to leave early. And my two sous-chefs helped."

Nathan cocked his head. "Drake and Mark. Those boys love to be in the kitchen."

"Yes. Martin tends to eat more than anyone else. He blames it on his athleticism, but he's going to be the last person to help in the kitchen."

"Have I told you I love you today?"

A giggle escaped me. This man had me feeling like a young woman again. "I love you. And I'm so proud of you. You were awesome today on the morning show. Lights and cameras agree with you."

"Thank you, I appreciate that. I was really nervous before we got started. I'm excited people are showing interest in The Assist Group. And after the show today, I don't know how he knew, but Drex left me a message to call him back. You know me and him haven't really talked, but I appreciate him wanting to endorse the program. It will go a long way since he is the most popular point guard in the NBA right now."

"That would be awesome. I know you want the program to expand nationally. You're off to a good start hitting the southeast cities like Charlotte, Atlanta, and Columbia. I guess since Drex transferred to the Miami Heat that will bring in a connection in Florida, right?"

"Yep. I'm excited about how things are coming together. But right now I'm more focused on other things."

He drew me closer.

"How am I supposed to finish dinner?"

"Just one kiss, as the appetizer."

"You do know my boys and your mom and sister are not that far away from the kitchen."

"And..."

We locked lips.

The doorbell rang, breaking our kiss.

I pulled back to catch my breath. "Were you expecting anyone else tonight?'

Nathan shook his head, his face a mask of frustration. "No, it's just my mom and Nadia.

Nadia's voice boomed from the other room. "What are you doing here?"

I glanced at Nathan, wondering who Nadia would be that rude to.

Nathan moved his long legs out of the kitchen. I peered at the clock, hoping whatever drama had appeared at the front of the house would make its exit. I reached into the cabinets to grab plates and salad bowls.

"Mom."

With my arms full, I saw Drake standing in the doorway. "Hey, sweetie, help me get these on the table. We should be eating in a bit."

Drake turned around nervously, and then headed in my direction. He took the salad bowls out of my hand. "Mom, someone is here."

I looked at the panic on my son's face and forgot about setting the table. I put the dishes in my arms on the counter behind me. Something was going on. As I left the kitchen with Drake on my heels, I could hear Nadia yelling.

"She has some nerve showing her face. Tell her to leave, Nate."

Nate.

Nadia and her mother sometimes called Nathan, Nate, an old endearing nickname from childhood. Usually something emotional was going on when his mom and sister turned to childhood names.

When I entered the alcove doorway leading into the living room, the first thing I noticed was how hushed the room went at my appearance. I had that creepy feeling you get when you have been the subject of the room. But in this case, I didn't think I was the subject.

That's when I caught a familiar face. A face I'd just seen earlier today. Someone who really was a stranger, but by the stress on Nathan's face was someone he knew. Also, someone who had Nadia standing with her fists tight like she was going into a fighter pose. Nathan's mother had her hands over her chest as if she was trying to keep her heart from leaping out.

I entered the room, conscience of Drake still at my elbow as if he was protecting me.

I smiled, though I didn't feel anything but fear crawling the length of my back. There were times when you knew the rug was about to be pulled out from under you and all you could do was lean on God to catch you when you fell.

I faced the woman. "So, we meet again. I didn't catch your name earlier today at the salon."

She smiled back at me, but the smile didn't reach her eyes, green eyes that I'd come to think weren't really contact lenses. She stepped forward, prompting Nathan to move in my direction. His eyes were hostile, a look I'd never seen on him.

"I'm sorry I didn't introduce myself earlier. You were busy. I'm Autumn Warner-Armstrong. Nathan and I... Well, we've known each other a long time."

Armstrong. Is she related to Drex Armstrong?

All kinds of bells started going off in my head. Now I knew why she seemed familiar to me. "I see. So you're the one who broke Nathan's heart."

I hope this woman didn't plan on stepping back into his life.

Chapter Three

After my statement, silence swept over the room. I was shocked by Autumn showing up at Nathan's house. Clearly, Nathan, his sister and mother were not pleased to see her. What angered me even more was the fact that she'd been in my salon earlier today.

What kind of game was this woman playing?

Nathan's initiative had been gathering some publicity but it wasn't the kind to dig up exes from the past. In particular, an ex-fiancée who conveniently dumped a man who no longer fit into her basketball wife scenario.

I turned to Nathan. "Would you like me to set a place at the table for Autumn? I didn't realize she was coming for family dinner tonight."

Nathan eyed me before turning to glare at Autumn. "She wasn't invited. And I'm not really sure why she's here now. Wait, you went to see Tangie earlier today. Why?"

Autumn shrugged as if the question was pure nonsense. "Well, I needed to find a salon. My hair was a mess. Crown of Beauty had rave reviews on Yelp, so I decided to start there." She turned towards me, and shook her head from side to side, making her hair flutter around her face. "You have a beautiful salon and your stylist was the best I've had in a long time."

"I'm glad we could help you today." I passed a look with Nathan. "I need to get dinner on the table. I'm sure everyone is hungry. Nadia, can you come help me?"

Normally, I wouldn't ask Nadia to do anything, but she looked like she was about to explode more than I was. Knowing how protective Nadia was of her brother, I believed if given a chance she would have wrapped her hands around Autumn's neck. What I needed at the moment was for everyone to be calm. My boys were here tonight and I didn't want anyone to let their emotions get the best of them.

Including me.

I took Drake by the elbow and propelled him out of the living room. "Where are your brothers?"

"They're playing the game. Why is that woman here?"

"I don't know the answer to that, but Nathan will deal with her. Go get your brothers and let them know we will eat soon."

I watched as Drake sprinted down the hallway ready to rile his brothers up about the unexpected visitor, no doubt. I entered the kitchen and grabbed the plates again. My mind was flowing with question after question. Why was she here? Why did she have the audacity to show up at my salon today? I wasn't buying the whole I needed some hair assistance thing. If she looked my salon up on Yelp, it wasn't by chance.

As I recalled our conversation earlier, it was clear the woman was there to check up on me. Check out who'd taken her place. From my understanding, she let Nathan go because she had no intentions of living her life with a man who'd lost his basketball career due to an injury.

Nadia came bursting through the door. "What are you doing?"

I scowled. "I'm getting dinner ready. You do want to eat?"

Nadia slapped her hands on the counter. "You need to tell her to go. And what's that mess about her showing up at your salon. Did you know it was her?"

I sighed. "I didn't know who she was. My salon takes walk-ins all the time."

"That woman is up to something. You know what she did to Nathan."

"I'm aware she walked away after he was injured."

"Walked away and stomped on his heart. They were together for three years. He thought she was the one for him, but he was so wrong. I could see the kind of woman she was from a mile away."

"Thanks for letting me know that, Nadia." I snapped. I grabbed the salad bowls and handed them to her. "Can you kindly assist me in getting the food on the table? I'm sure your mama and the kids are ready to eat. Nathan will handle Autumn."

Nadia grabbed the bowls but stood staring at me. "You need to take this seriously. That's the most manipulative woman I've ever met. She's bad news, I'm telling you. If Nathan doesn't deal with her, I will." With that, she marched out into the dining room. I could hear her slamming the poor salad bowls down on the table. All this time

I thought Nadia didn't care for me. But there was someone else she didn't care for even more. I wasn't sure how to feel about that.

Dinner was eaten in silence. Normally, my boys were talkative, but Drake must have delivered the news to Martin and Mark, who both kept throwing me furtive glances as if they were afraid their Mama would fall apart. It also didn't help that Nathan hadn't arrived at the dinner table. I assumed he would get rid of Autumn, but he didn't. In fact, when I checked outside, his car was gone.

So we all finished our meal. Both Nadia and Nathan's mom helped me clear the table. I turned to both of them. "Thank you, both."

Monica was a quiet woman compared to her daughter Nadia. I suspected Nadia took after her dad while Nathan's quiet, calm demeanor was more like his mother. She asked, "Are you okay? You're an awfully strong woman to continue to feed us and make sure everyone else is okay?"

"It's what I do, Mrs. Chambers. I don't know what else to do."

Monica smiled. "Monica, just call me Monica. And I know. I did that too with my kids. Keep things normal and protect them from the world.

I'm glad you are being calm, Tangie. Please trust my Nathan. He will handle *this* woman."

"I'm not worried. Though I am concerned about her showing up at my salon today. What was her motive other than to check me out? It makes me wonder how long she's been keeping an eye on me and Nathan."

Monica observed me. "Yes, that's a concern. But it's how she got Nathan. She was one of those groupies, always showing up at interesting times."

I eyed her. "She's married to Drex Armstrong, correct? Nathan is trying to get Drex to endorse The Assist Group. Maybe we are all overreacting and she's here on her husband's behalf."

Monica's eyes held pity. "Child, I'm old but even I keep up with things on Facebook. And it's not even just Facebook, it's been on that *Entertainment News*. They broke up a few weeks ago. Drex filed for a divorce. That woman may think she can get my Nate back."

"Oh."

That wasn't good.

I used to keep up with social media but as my boys got older, it had become impossible. With Martin needing to be at basketball practice, Mark in band competitions and lately, Drake in robotics competitions, it was enough to keep up with my co-ownership of the salon. And the past few months I'd been knee deep in wedding planning and still way behind.

After Monica left the kitchen, I pulled my phone out of my back pocket. I quickly typed Drex Armstrong in the browser's search bar.

Sure enough there were stories and reporters talking about the breakup. My eyes caught one story that mentioned Autumn had dated and been engaged to former NBA player, Nathan Chambers.

Great!

Right now my fiancé was somewhere talking to his former fiancée who'd just been served divorce papers by her current NBA husband.

What's next?

Nathan returned just as I finished stacking dishes in the dishwasher. Martin drove him and his brothers back to our home while I waited around for Nathan's return. I didn't make a habit of staying too late over at Nathan's place. We decided a long time ago to remain celibate until our wedding night. It was hard, but there was no need to stoke the fires of temptation.

Unfortunately tonight, there was no way I was going home without seeing Nathan in person. I had to know why he didn't send Autumn away and instead brushed off the family meal to talk to her. I'd been trying to be cool about it, but now I was fuming.

This woman had been living the life and now that her NBA player husband had filed for divorce, she came running back to Nathan. That's not how this worked. There were plenty of other fish in the basketball sea for her to pursue. She was clearly pretty enough to draw attention.

I'd been reading social media posts and comments about what people were saying. Interesting, the comments were 50-50. Some comments that sided with Drex were mainly women.

taylor1234: *She's always been a gold digger. Remember how she left Nathan Chambers when he got injured.*

SusanGee: *I heard she cheated on Drex. Of course she did. Everybody knows she was stepping out on Nathan Chambers. That's why she dropped him so fast. Girl had her somebody in the wings.*

But there were some comments on Autumn's side. Also mainly women.

LaylaH: *Drex Armstrong is a dog! I'm surprised he even married her. Probably because of that little boy. He dotes on that child.*

MissLuv98: *He's definitely a player. I remember him from high school. That man ain't never gonna change. I heard he had side chicks the whole time they'd been married.*

I finally stopped reading the comments. All of it was gossip. When I was younger, and a lot more arrogant, I spouted my opinions off with the best of them. But as a single mother of three sons, I had my share of haters, especially since becoming attached to Nathan. Besides, nobody knew what went on in a couple's private life. What I did know, Autumn had made her way into my life and I didn't like it at all.

I heard the front door open and sat up on the couch from where I'd been laying. Nathan came into the living room. His head drooped and his face shattered. "Are you okay?"

He slumped down on the couch next to me. Without hesitation, despite the risks, I hugged him tight, leaning into his chest. His muscles were taut; his breath shallow like he'd been working out. I leaned back to peer at his face. "What happened?"

He swallowed. "Can I get that dinner I missed? I will tell you all about it. I promise."

"Sure." We both rose from the couch, my hand in his. He held my hand tightly until we arrived in the kitchen. Then he pulled a chair out and slumped down like an old man. I tried to hide my concern by grabbing the pan of chicken and salad from the fridge. While the chicken heated, I mixed up the salad all the while keeping an eye on Nathan. He reminded me of someone in shock; his eyes were unfocused. I wondered if he knew where he was and that I was nearby fixing his dinner.

I was officially scared. I'd never seen him like this before.

I set the plate in front of Nathan along with a glass of ice tea. We sat in silence as Nathan sliced up the grilled chicken and placed it over his salad. He'd drenched the salad with the Italian dressing like he always did. He must have been starving; the salad was demolished in no time.

He pushed the plate to the side. "I guess Mama and Nadia left a while ago."

"Yes, they left over an hour ago when the boys left. It's pretty late and I probably should head home. I didn't want to leave without ... seeing you."

Nathan stared at me through glazed eyes. "Do you mind staying a bit longer? I will make sure you get home safely. I know you trust the boys on their own, but I also know you like to be there with them too."

I smiled despite the nervous ache gliding through my abdomen. "Sounds serious. We can wait until the morning."

He frowned. "Aren't you going to the bridal shop in the morning?"

"You remember." I joked.

"We're getting married. I try to remember the details, though they can be a lot sometimes."

I took a deep breath. "You want to talk about Autumn? I read about her and Drex."

He nodded. "Yes, they separated a few weeks ago. Drex and I hadn't spoken in years, although I have been focused on getting him to become a part of The Assist Group. He's a popular player and a lot of young kids look up to him. Plus, a lot of people don't know this but Drex has two siblings who are engineers."

"Wow. I see why you reached out to him."

The kitchen had been a comfortable temperature, but I felt a chill as silence enveloped the room again. "Nathan, I don't want to pry, but what did you talk to Autumn about? It's kind of crazy her showing up at my salon."

Nathan frowned. "Yeah. I'm sorry. I don't know what she thought she was doing. Believe me she heard me loud and clear to stay away from you, but…"

I tilted my head. "Why is there a but?"

"It's going to be hard to ignore Autumn. She told me something tonight that she should have told me four years ago."

I leaned on the table; my eyes fixed on Nathan. "She was keeping a secret."

"Yeah, a big one. A life changing secret."

In my head, Nathan's words echoed.

Life changing?

"When she broke up with me, she failed to tell me that she was pregnant."

Pregnant.

At first I wasn't sure I heard Nathan correctly. "Did you say she was pregnant?"

"Yeah, all this time I thought Noah was Drex's son. But he's not. He's mine."

I opened my mouth to respond, but words escaped me. As I waited for Nathan to return tonight, I had read somewhere on the social media posts that Autumn and Drex had a son. Some had speculated that's why Drex, the ultimate bad boy, married her. I even saw Drex holding a little boy in a few photos.

I stared at Nathan. "That's why Drex broke up with her. He found out the little boy isn't his. He's your son."

Nathan has a son.

Chapter Four

Nathan has a son. Autumn wasn't going any-where. She would be a factor in our lives forever. Nathan said he would be taking a paternity test before he met the boy, but last night before going to bed I searched online for photos. There were only a few. Apparently Drex and Autumn tried to keep the boy out of the spotlight. The few I found, Drex held the young boy on his shoulders or in his arms. As I stared at the child, his big brown eyes reminded me of a photo Nathan's mother kept in the living room of the house where Nathan grew up.

This boy was the spitting image of Nathan.

All this time, how come no one noticed?

And how could Autumn not realize Nathan was the father?

I couldn't fathom how a woman would deny a man his own child. Was it so important for Autumn to be a basketball wife that she'd deny a child his true father? Or did she not know? Maybe after she broke up with Nathan, she didn't have the heart to tell him. Either way, she destroyed two men's lives, one who'd been the father all this time and one who never knew he was father.

This little boy would be so confused. My heart broke for him.

"Tangie, Tangie, are you alright?"

I blinked my eyes, focusing on where I was standing. There were rows of white. White dresses and hanging nearby were lavender bridesmaid dresses. I was supposed to be concentrating on picking out my wedding dress and the bridesmaid dresses this morning.

I stared down at the dress I was wearing and then turned my attention to the mirror. It was an off the shoulder dress, hanging just below my knees. It was beautiful but it wasn't calling my name. None of the dresses had been this morning. I glanced in the mirror at the reflection of a group of women behind me. Four sets of eyes waited with expectancy and concern. The sight of Candace, Nadia, Beulah Samuels and Lenora made tears blur my eyes. All of this emotion and it had nothing to do with the dress. I was going to disappoint all of them again. The fourth time in the last hour.

What a wasted Saturday morning.

I turned around and took a breath. "Sorry, I zoned out there. Lenora, this is a beautiful dress but..."

Lenora reached for my hand. "It's not the one. But it fits you so perfectly. Doesn't need that much fitting. Are you okay, sweetie? Maybe we should reschedule the fitting. You just don't seem to be into any of the dresses we chose for you today."

"That's because she's probably in shock." Nadia commented.

I glared at my future sister-in-law, but then realized she was right despite her outburst. Besides, I was sure the news Nathan shared with me last night hit Nadia and his mother just as hard. They'd been denied their nephew and grandson.

A mini-Nathan.

Beulah touched my arm. "Shock about what? Tangie, what's going on?"

I'd been keeping it together, but Beulah's presence reminded me how much I missed my mama. The unshed tears made their descent down my face.

"Oh, no," Candace pulled tissues out of her purse. "Honey, are you having wedding jitters?"

"Can you blame her?" Nadia folded her arms.

Beulah stared at Nadia. "What did your brother do?"

Nadia placed her hands on her hips. "My brother didn't do anything. It's that other woman, his former fiancée that came and crashed his world. She broke his heart and then had the nerve..."

"Nadia," I shouted. "Please."

Nadia shut her mouth and had the decency to look ashamed.

I took in a breath and wiped the corners of my eyes. "Look, you all might as well know. It's going to come out. Lenora, help me out of this dress. You're right, my head isn't here today for this. I'm sorry I wasted all your time."

Back in the dressing room. I slid out of the dress and hung it back on the satin hanger. I stared at it for a moment. It was a beautiful dress, but how could I think about a wedding right now? Back in my tunic and leggings, I felt slightly better but not much. A headache had started to loom and I wanted my bed. But I also owed everyone an explanation.

We all ended up in Lenora's office in the back of the bridal shop. It was a good size room with a sitting area that included a couch and chairs. Lenora brought out a tea pot.

Everyone sat and chatted about other things while I sipped my tea. It was a strong brew of cinnamon and ginger. In a way, it cleared my senses. "I'm ready to talk. Y'all heard of Drex Armstrong?"

Lenora nodded. "Reverend Freeman and my sons are basketball fans. They love him. He's been in the news lately. Him and his wife are getting a divorce. That's not what has you down, Tangie. I know it seems like people don't stay together anymore, but they do."

Beulah nodded. "Yes, they do. All the things going on in the world and the media has nothing better to do than report on somebody's love life. What does he have to do with anything?"

I gripped my hands. "Well, the woman Drex broke up with is Nathan's former fiancée. Autumn Warner. She showed up yesterday. In fact, she was at the salon yesterday morning."

Candace held her hands over her chest. "What? She came to our salon. For what? Was she spying on you or something?"

"I have no idea. But she showed up later at Nathan's house and dropped a bomb on him."

Beulah asked. "Child, what could she have possibly said? Didn't you say she broke up with him?"

"Yeah, but she failed to tell him she was pregnant at the time."

Candace, Lenora and Beulah jumped back in their seats like they'd been punched.

Nadia tossed her locs over her shoulder. "Told you my brother didn't do anything. This woman decided upon herself to kick him when he'd already been hurt and had to give up his career. She got the nerve to pretend like another man was the father of her child. I don't know the full story, but it explains why Drex kicked her out of his house. It's a shame."

Candace held her hand on the side of her face. "What about the boy? So, Drex is just going to leave him. And is Nathan really sure? Shouldn't he take a paternity test?"

Nadia smacked her hands on her lap. "Yes, he's going to take a test, but there's no denying that boy is Nathan's son. Now why she waited this long, I don't know. But the boy is still young."

"Noah," I stated softly.

Candace turned to me. "Tangie, what did you say?"

I cleared my throat. "The boy's name is Noah. Noah Armstrong."

Nadia pointed at me. "You mean Noah Chambers. My brother will straighten all of this out. He's going to get his boy back. The only problem is going to be that mama of his. Autumn didn't just decide to do this. Drex probably forced her hand. He will probably divorce her and all that money she was after, she won't get dime. I heard he has a prenup. Good thing too!"

I frowned. "How do you know this?"

"Nathan told us. Apparently, Autumn is about to lose everything and she's come to dangle that boy, sorry, Noah in my brother's face. She's just hoping she can inch her way into his money. Nathan might have lost his basketball career, but he had good senses with his finances. It's why he was able to get his foundation off the ground on his own before getting other NBA players to pledge their support."

I knew all about Nathan's finances. It's why he had such an elaborate home, but that's where he stopped. He didn't drive a fancy vehicle and worked as a guidance counselor at The Lab. He really was all about using his money to help others. It's one of the reasons why I loved him.

Beulah looked at me and then back at Nadia. "Why are you talking like this? Tangie is already upset about the situation and we know Nathan loves her."

Nadia turned to me like she'd really just noticed me. "I know my brother loves you, but Autumn is a manipulator. Believe me, you're going to have to watch your back. It might pay for you to postpone the wedding."

Lenora and Candace both stood, protesting.

Nadia held up her hands. "I'm just saying. Autumn is the kind of woman who'd find a way to mess up the wedding. Don't take my word for it. You said she showed up at your salon yesterday. She's watching you, Tangie. Mark my words. Nathan needs to get his son from her and that woman has got to go."

The other women argued with Nadia. I hated to hear what she was saying, but I also sensed some truth.

I hoped and prayed Autumn had a change of heart and was doing what was best for her son. But I knew I needed to watch my back too.

Chapter Five

Nathan took a paternity test the following Monday and told me the results would be ready in five days. I hadn't mentioned anything to my sons, so those felt like the longest five days I'd experienced in some time. It was hard to keep quiet, but I felt like it was Nathan's story to tell when he was ready. By the end of the week, the paternity test results confirmed what everyone already knew. I looked as emotions warred on Nathan's face as he re-read the paper again.

"You have to get him." Nathan's mama cried. She'd been softly crying since Nathan opened the envelope. "How could she keep your son, my grandson from me? What a horrible woman!"

Nadia rubbed their mother's shoulders. "Mama's right. You need to get a lawyer. That woman needs to pay for what she's done."

I was happy that Nathan was a father. I knew how much he loved my boys. But Martin and Mark were seventeen-year-old, high school se-niors and Drake would be turning twelve soon. They were not babies. And even though they all got along great with Nathan, I often wondered if I could have another child. It'd been almost twelve years and I was no spring chicken. Though he never said anything, I would imagine Nathan thought about having a kid together with me. There was something about a newborn, starting over with a new life, boy or girl.

I sometimes thought about how nice it would be to have a girl. All of these thoughts bom-barded me. I pushed them down because they weren't important. I thought about what Nadia said about postponing the wedding. Now wasn't the time. My heart hurt. I felt Nathan's pain; so much time had passed without knowing he had a son. He'd missed out on some of the milestones, but Nathan could be there for Noah's first day of school and even put him in a Pee Wee sports game if the little man was so inclined.

Nadia took their mother home. After walking his mother and sister to the car, Nathan returned inside and our eyes met. I got up from the chair in the corner where I'd been sitting. I'm not sure why, but when Nathan opened the envelope, I felt like I needed to let him and his family have the moment. He insisted that I stay. Now he looked at me, his eyes pleading.

"What are you thinking, Tangie Nelson? You've been quiet."

I cleared my throat. "It's a lot to take in. I just want to be here for you. I can't imagine how you feel."

"I'm not sure how I feel. I'm kind of numb right now, but I've had periods of anger and sadness. And it doesn't help that Drex has been calling me. I haven't had the heart to pick up the phone. What do I say to him? He thought the world of Noah. *His* son."

"Maybe you should pick up the phone next time. He may just want to talk and make sure Noah will be alright. The next thing would be for you to meet Noah, right?"

Nathan took a breath, sucking in air like it hurt his lungs. "He's here in Charlotte. Autumn didn't think it best to see him yet. But he has to have questions about what's going on. And you know Mama and Nadia want to see him too."

At that moment the doorbell rang.

Nathan glanced towards the door.

I looked at the time. It was almost eight o'clock and I should be heading home. "Were you expecting someone?" I prayed it wasn't Autumn. I didn't think I could look that woman in the face right now.

Nathan looked at the phone app that let him see visitors at his door. I meant to ask him how it felt that night seeing Autumn again after so much time. But then I came to my senses. Did I really want to know how my fiancé felt about his ex?

Nathan lifted his head to look at me; his eyebrow furrowed. "It's Drex. He's been trying to call me but I didn't think he would find me."

"He's never been to your house?"

"No, remember we haven't been in touch in years. I bought this house after I left basketball, but he knows I went back to my hometown."

I stood from the couch. "Oh, well, I should leave you two to talk."

"No, I want you to stay."

I frowned, not sure if it would be a good idea for the two men to have an audience. Nathan was in an emotional state and for Drex to show up at his house, that couldn't be a good thing. I sat back down and clasped my hands in my lap. My nerves were on edge as Nathan answered the door.

From where I sat, I couldn't see the man, but I heard his voice. "Nate. Hey, I hope this isn't a bad time."

"What's up, Drex?"

"I've been trying to call you and I figured since I was passing through Charlotte, I might as well see you. It's been a long time, man."

"Yeah, it has been a long time. Sorry for missing your calls. I have been wanting to touch base more about The Assist Group."

"Aw, you know I'm in. Anything for the kids."

"Good."

I looked up, feeling self-conscience about listening to the conversation. Drex appeared around the corner and stopped when he saw me. He was slightly taller than Nathan. The men shared similar complexions, but that's where their similarities stopped. Drex's hair was dyed blond at the top where tiny twists sat on the top of his head. He wore an earring in both ears and I could see tattoos rising up from his shirt collar around his neck. I'd seen photos of Drex, many in recent days. He had tattoos over most of his body.

"Oh, man. I'm sorry. I should have known you had company. Look, we can do this some other time."

Nathan glanced at me; his nervousness palpable. "It's fine. You can talk in front of Tangie. Tangie, this is Drex Armstrong. Drex, this is my fiancée Tangie Nelson."

Drex grinned at Nate before turning back to me. "Yeah, you're finally getting hitched. Congratulations. This is Martin's mom, right?"

I raised an eyebrow wondering how an NBA star knew my son.

Nathan chuckled. "Yes. Tangie has three wonderful boys. She's done a good job with all of them."

"Hello, Drex. It's good to meet you. And I take it you met my oldest son?"

Drex stepped into the room. "Yes, ma'am. That boy has some skills. I was down in Charlotte for the championship game before the holidays. He's good. I definitely see him getting drafted to an NBA team in a few years."

"Thank you. That's his dream. I want to make sure his head doesn't get too big so he can graduate high school first."

Drex threw his head back and laughed. "I hear that. You remind me of my mom."

Nathan came to stand beside me. "Hey, man. Have a seat. Can I get you anything?"

The elephant in the room seemed to grow bigger despite Drex's jubilant attitude. I could almost feel the shift in the conversation before it started.

"No, I'm good." Drex sat on the leather loveseat across from us, while we resumed sitting on the couch.

"I don't want to hold y'all up, but I was trying to call you to warn you about something."

Nathan glanced at me. "I think I already know. We've seen Autumn."

Drex let out a few explicit words, making my ears burn. "Sorry, man. I don't know what to say other than I didn't know. I miss the little dude, but I thought it best to stay away."

Nathan leaned forward. "I'm sorry too. I know how much you love Noah. Do you mind telling me how you found out? Autumn wasn't really forthcoming. She claimed she didn't know."

Drex let loose another string of cuss words. "Sorry for my French. Noah got sick! He had a lot of tests. Found out he was anemic. He needed a blood transfusion and the doctor made a statement about my blood type. He didn't say I couldn't be Noah's father but something in his face made me see he was thinking how is this possible. I did some thinking and it occurred to me a long time ago. But it's complicated, man. I know we were friends, man. I should have never crossed that line."

Crossed the line. Oh no!

I was growing uncomfortable by the second. Autumn may not have really known who the father was if she'd been cheating on Nathan with his friend.

Nathan coughed. "It's past history now. I just want to do what's right for Noah."

Drex sighed. "Have you seen him?"

"No, I'm hoping to this weekend. My mom and sister really are anxious."

"Oh, yeah. I bet. I remember your mom and your sister. Nadia, right? She's a firecracker."

"My family is not too pleased about what Autumn has done."

Drex's nose flared; his eyes filled with pain. "I can't deal with her right now. I haven't told my family about what's going on. Everyone is all upset about me filing for divorce, but I can't tell them. Noah has been my son for four years. I don't know if he's going to understand."

Nathan swallowed. "We will take it slow. I don't want you to think you have to not be in his life. The most important thing is to protect Noah."

Drex looked away, licking his lips. "I agree. Let me know when you want to see Noah. I'm trying to avoid Autumn. Maybe it would be better for you to meet him without her around."

Nathan tilted his head to the side. "If you think that's best."

Drex stood. "I think she will try to confuse things. You need to watch out for Autumn. I wouldn't trust her. It still burns me up. If Noah hadn't gotten sick, I would have never known. She didn't even bother to confirm who his real dad was even though... Let's just say Autumn has always been sneaky."

Nathan rose from the couch with his hands clenched. "Thanks for the heads up."

Both men stared at each other, unspoken words seemed to linger between them. Nathan finally held his hand out and they shook hands.

Drex turned to me. "It was nice meeting you. I know Noah will be in good hands seeing how you raised your own boys."

I nodded, finding unexpected emotions rising to the surface. Not once had I even thought about my influence on this young boy I'd never met. Indeed, when Nathan and I married, it was possible we would have a young boy become a part of our family.

His mother would be there too.

Nathan closed the door and leaned against it. His eyes were unfocused.

"Are you okay? This is a lot to process."

"Yeah, it is." He walked back over to the couch.

"Did you know Autumn was cheating on you?"

Nathan leaned his head back against the couch and stared up at the ceiling. "It didn't occur to me until her and Drex hooked up. It seemed to happen so fast. Then I heard she had a baby. In my mind, I figured she broke up with me because she was having his child. I never imagined she was carrying mine."

"It sounds like Drex is not going to be able to let go as easily as he wants. I saw some photos of him with Noah on his IG profile."

"Yeah. I know. I want to meet him and be a part of his life, but I don't know how to navigate this mess. I don't want to see Noah ... my son traumatized by his mother's decision."

I moved in closer on the couch and put my arms around Nathan. "I'm glad that you and Drex will work this out together, making sure Noah's protected."

Nathan leaned his head against mine.

Drex's warnings echoed in my mind.

You need to watch out for Autumn.

Autumn had managed to disrupt all of our lives. I wanted Nathan to have a relationship with his son, but I wasn't sure if I could handle whatever Autumn was bringing to the table.

Chapter Six

At the beginning of the week, Drex's warning hit home. I was in the salon office unpacking supplies when Candace came up to me with her phone in her hand. Immediately, I knew something was wrong; Candace always had a calm demeanor. At the sight of her wide eyes, I dropped the bottle of conditioner back into the box.

"What? What's going on?" Hysteria rose in my voice and my body as if she'd stepped in the office yelling the salon was on fire. I'd been on edge the entire weekend, often scolding myself about my old the sky is falling habit that had crept into my mind the past week.

"Look at this." Candace shoved her phone in front of me showing a social media post from Instagram.

I gave her the side eye but didn't say anything. Candace wasn't a social media type of person. We had a Facebook page and our stylists helped manage our Instagram profile by posting photos of clients and their hairstyles.

I took a look at the Instagram post and sucked in a breath. It was a picture of Autumn. She had a bluish-purple bruise down the side of her face, and her right eye appeared swollen. It looked like someone had gone to town on Autumn's face. But who? My mind went straight to Drex and the night he showed up at Nathan's house. His anger was contained but boiling under the surface. No one could blame him for loving a child all these years only to find out it wasn't his.

But would he harm the child's mother? He'd separated himself from them and both he and Nathan had agreed to protect Noah. Harming Autumn, no matter what she did, was not good for the child.

I noticed I wasn't looking at a photo, but a video where Autumn appeared to be talking on camera.

"What is she saying?" I pressed the button to play the video. I'd only heard Autumn's voice a few times, but I recognized her sultry tone, even though her face appeared quite the opposite.

"Hey, guys. I haven't been on here in a while. Things have been going really, really wrong in my life. As you know, Drex and I officially broke up. And I have to say, at first, I felt scared about the breakup. But then, I felt relief. And I thought well, I can move on with my life. But my ex and I have a difference of opinion. He still wants to control me even though he doesn't want me anymore.

"I don't want to make Drex look bad, but I need the world to know I can no longer have him around my son. I just ask that you all pray for me. Pray for us. That we can all get through this. I will be off social media for a little while longer because I have a lot to think about. Things have to change."

I sat for a moment kind of stunned, and then I looked at Candace who shared a similar look of confusion. I told Candace about Drex coming to the house and what he and Nathan had talked about.

"I'm not sure how to interpret this video. She didn't come right out and say Drex hit her, but she definitely made it seem like he was responsible."

Candace crossed her arms. "She did lie to the man about the boy. Or at least she didn't bother to confirm the boy's paternity, knowing she had been unfaithful. But still, I don't like a man hitting a woman."

I agreed. "Drex did warn us not to trust her. Nadia has been griping about her being manipulative. I honestly don't know what to think. But this video on social media is not a good look for Drex. It's gonna be the talk and they were already in the spotlight for the divorce."

"He could face criminal charges for this too." Candace mentioned.

"That would ruin his career." I handed Candace back her phone.

Candace placed the phone on the desk and turned back to me. "How are you doing with all of this, Tangie? I haven't heard you talk about the wedding. Did you reschedule the wedding dress fitting with Lenora?"

I stood from the couch and paced as much as the small office would allow. "I have put all that out of my mind for now. We have more important things to worry about besides wedding planning. It just doesn't seem to be a good idea. Besides, Nathan has been preparing himself to meet his son."

"Are you going to go with him?"

I shook my head. "No, it doesn't feel right. It's going to be too much on a little boy. And besides that, I haven't told my boys. I only told you and Beulah. Of course Nadia and Nathan's mom knows, but it's very few people. Nathan wasn't even sure if they should say anything to Noah yet. You know, just start out by him getting to know them."

Candace nodded. "Poor baby. Yes, that makes sense. The good thing is he's still young. He can get to know Nathan as well as keep his relationship with Drex. But I have to say if Drex really put his hand on the boy's mom, that's going to make things even more difficult in the future."

The office phone rang and Candace picked up. She frowned and handed the phone to me. "It's Drake."

I frowned and looked at the time. It was still another hour before Drake left school. He should be with his robotics group right now. "Drake. Are you okay? Where are you?"

"I'm here at school. A lot of kids are saying crazy things about Nathan. I tried to go to his office to see him, but he wasn't there."

I glanced at Candace who was looking at me intently. "Oh, what are people saying?"

"There's a picture of Nathan and that lady that came to the house. And she's all over social media and her face is messed up. Some people think

Drex hit her. People are saying Drex was mad because she went back to Nathan. But that's not true because you and Nathan are getting married."

I swallowed the lump of fear that seemed stuck to my vocal cords. "Of course it's not true. Nathan will explain what's going on soon. Are you going to your robotics club?"

"No, I want to go home."

"Alright, I will pick you up."

I hung up the phone and looked at Candace. "I don't know what's going on, but Nathan's name is appearing somewhere on social media. Some photo with Autumn. Drake's upset. I need to go get him." I sighed deeply. "If Drake heard something, that means Martin and Mark did too. And you know how they all feel about Nathan."

"You should get Nathan to set the record straight. They need to hear from him."

"Before I go anywhere, I need us to pray."

The salon office was so much more on many occasions. Right now, as Candace grabbed my hand, the quietness of the office transported it into a prayer room.

Dear Lord,

I don't understand what's going on, but I know you do. I know you see things at work that we can't see with our naked eye. We're praying that you will protect all involved, especially a young boy who's at the center. We pray healing for his mother as well as the men who've been emotionally affected. Lord, please provide me the strength to be there for my family, to be a support system for Nathan and his family. We ask for all these things in Jesus name. Amen.

Candace hugged me. "It's going to be okay, Tangie. Know that whatever is going on, God is in control of the situation."

I grabbed my bag and left the salon. Before I got in my car, I dialed Nathan's phone number. It rang and rang. Once inside the car, I heard Nathan's voicemail kick in.

"Where are you, Nathan? Look, Drake is upset. I'm sure Martin and Mark may be too. Something is going on and I need to hear from you. Please call me back."

For the first time I started to wonder if there was something I had missed. In the video that I saw, Autumn never came right out and identified the person who assaulted her. But it was clear she was insinuating Drex had something to do with it.

Where was this photo that implicated Nathan getting back with Autumn?

I didn't know Drex, but I knew Nathan. Over the past year, I'd seen how he treated his mother, his sister and me. I'd seen the care he'd taken with my sons. I watched and admired over the past few weeks how he still looked out for a boy he'd never met, being sensitive to not rock his son's world.

Even more important, Nathan was a God-fearing man who had no shame in letting the world know he loved the Lord.

Before pulling out of the parking lot, I went back to Autumn's Instagram profile. All I found was the video I'd already seen.

I did a search and found the photo in question. It was posted on the Nessa B blog. She was an infamous blogger who also had a podcast. Her main objective was all about spilling the beans on celebrities. A Wendy Williams wanna be, Nessa had a very short-lived career as a rapper but fizzled after one hit. That didn't stop her from enjoying the spotlight. She'd created this show a few years ago which hosted other artists, mostly B-list actresses and athletes, in particular wives and girlfriends of athletes.

She was also the first one to snap and post a photo of me and Nathan out in public. Through other people, I'd since been made aware of her insistence on posting about me, but I had no dirt to give her.

Someone must have snapped the photo when Autumn was telling Nathan the news. I could see the look of hurt and betrayal on his face. Why would Autumn reveal something like that to Nathan in such a public place?

I read through the blog post as Nessa made her insinuation about this meeting between "former lovers." Then, I noticed an interview segment.

Autumn talked to this pariah.

I looked at the date the interview posted. It was a few days before Autumn arrived at my salon for the first time. I could only imagine she was spilling the beans about her and Drex's breakup. But why? Why would people put their personal business out for the world? Yes, she was married to one of the top basketball players in the NBA right now, but she had a son and she could absolutely keep her privacy.

I looked at the time, realizing I needed to pick up Drake soon. I needed to know where the rumors were coming from so I at least knew how to have a conversation with my boys. It also would be a good idea for Nathan to show up. It wasn't like him not to respond to my calls.

I pressed play on the interview, which was really a three-minute snippet.

Nessa B: I'm sorry to hear about you and Drex. We all have been pulling for you.

Autumn: "Thank you. It's been a hard few weeks, especially on my son, but sometimes things work out for the best."

Nessa B: "Is that so? You all seem so close. I don't think you ever missed a game."

Autumn grimaced. "It was required."

Nessa eyed Autumn. "Required. Girl, you sound like you were on lockdown."

Autumn smiled. "I can't talk too much, but I have a habit of being around toxic men.

Nessa moved her hands around. "Well, we all run into them sometimes. But you had some good ones. You were dating Nathan Chambers before Drex. I know that had to be awkward. Those two guys were tight."

Autumn bit her lip. "Everyone isn't what they seem. Two peas in a pod. Those two."

"I don't know. They seemed kind of opposite to me. Drex is the bad boy, and Nathan comes off like a choir boy to me."

That's because he is, I thought.

I stopped the video. I couldn't take seeing anymore. Why was Autumn on this show talking about her relationship? And how dare she paint a picture of Nathan like this. She was the one who dumped him and had the nerve to pass his child off on another man.

Just a few minutes ago I was torn about seeing the damage on Autumn's face. The more I stared at her eyes, I realized it was the same look I saw when she was at the salon and later when she showed up at Nathan's house. There was a slyness in her expression and a slight smirk to her lips as she faced the camera.

What was it that Nadia said?

That's the most manipulative woman I've ever met.

I stuffed my phone into my bag and pulled out of the parking lot. "What are you doing, Autumn?"

Chapter Seven

When I arrived home, I knew something was wrong. With a house full of boys, quiet often equaled trouble. With long strides, I headed to the heart of the house, the kitchen. Every afternoon, I would find the refrigerator and the cabinets ransacked. Three growing boys kept me making trips to the grocery store. But recently, I'd been skipping the store all together and getting pantry items delivered from online or requesting a shopper. I could see from the open cabinet that it was time to make another order.

"Well, I see you all are home. I hope you didn't ruin your appetites for dinner."

Martin looked at me. "Have you heard?"

I peered at Drake, who came in behind me. He'd been upset, close to the point of tears. His eyes were still sorrowful and red like his world had come crashing down.

Though I was fairly certain I knew what the twins knew, I asked. "Hear what?"

Martin held up his phone so I could see Autumn's bruised face. "Wasn't she at Nathan's house the other night? Why did he leave to go with her?"

I started to open my mouth, but then realized I hadn't told my boys anything. They had no idea why Nathan left. Since they hadn't asked, I figured they'd forgotten about it.

Mark was the quiet twin. He and Drake were both sensitive boys and took things to heart. Not afraid to be blunt, Mark asked. "Did Nathan do this?"

"What? Of course not. Why would you think that?"

Mark shrugged casually, but his face was stony. "Because everyone could see how upset he was to see her. She used to be his fiancée until she dropped him."

"Has Nathan ever given you any reason to think he was violent?"

The boys all looked at each other. Martin spoke up, "No, but sometimes you can get mad about stuff and reach out in anger."

Drake cleared his throat. "I did that. That's how I got suspended." My youngest son had been bullied for some time at his old school, and even though he reached out to the adults around him, no one stepped in.

I pulled out a chair from the kitchen table and sat down. My body felt tired. "I saw that video. Candace showed it to me. You all know Autumn didn't say who touched her. If anything, she seemed to be implicating her husband who has filed divorce."

Martin leaned over and looked at me. "Yeah, I agree with that. But it doesn't explain why she went to Nathan's house. Mom, you and Nathan are together now."

Drake piped up. "Yes, you're getting married. She can't just show up like that."

I really wish I could tell the boys what was going on, but I knew my sons. They were too emotional right now and they all had friends they talked too. Nathan and Drex ultimately wanted to protect Noah so keeping his paternity issues out of the public was important.

"Trust me. Nathan would never hurt that woman. I don't think Drex did either. There is something going on, but I can't tell you too much right now. I can tell you that Drex and Nathan are working together to protect someone. I believe this will all work out soon."

All my boys stared back at me; skepticism written all over their faces. I couldn't blame them. Inside, I was struggling with fears and doubts because I had no idea what was going on. And I desperately needed to hear from Nathan. I had to know he was alright about everything going on.

Lately, I'd been reading novels before going to bed. I wasn't always a reader, but we had an author in our bible study at church. And after reading the latest novel from Nia Michaels, I decided to keep up the habit by first purchasing a Kindle. Since then, I'd loaded up several books.

This one was a mystery and I was trying to wrap my head around who did it. Probably the last thing I needed with all the mysteries up in the air in my own life. My phone rang from my nightstand. I peered over to see a photo of Nathan smiling back at me. I'd snapped the photo of him when we went to the beach this past summer. He was bare chested with a mischievous look in his eyes.

I answered the phone on the second ring. "Nathan."

"Hey, babe. I'm sorry it took me so long to get back to you."

"You had me worried. The boys are all upset about everything on social media. What happened to Autumn?"

Nathan sighed. "I wish I knew. What I do know is she's not letting me see Noah."

I sat up in bed. "What?"

"I've been trying to track her down all day. So has Drex. He did go over to see her last Friday after he stopped by my house. They had words, but he left when Noah woke up. He said he went over there to see Noah, but Autumn wouldn't let him."

"That's terrible. I'm sure the little boy is wondering what's going on. And why would she not let you see him now. She came to tell you about him. What was the point of all that?"

"I don't know."

"Did Drex do anything to her? He had plenty of reasons to be mad. And if she wasn't letting him see Noah, that could have set him off."

"Drex said he didn't put a hand on her. They yelled at each other, but that's all."

"Do you believe him?"

Nathan sighed deeply. "I want to. Drex does have a temper, and he has gotten into it with other guys. But I've never known him to hit a woman."

"This is all a shame. You could tell he's broken up about everything."

"I guess I need to get a lawyer. I was trying not to do that, you know. I just want to meet Noah and get to know him."

"Nathan?"

"Yeah, Tangie."

"Is it possible Autumn could be playing some game here? She's purposely keeping you and Drex away from Noah. It doesn't seem like very stable behavior."

"Well, something happened to her face. Do you think she did that to herself?"

"I don't know. But there was another interview. Have you seen the one she did on the Nessa B. show?"

"No, I'm not aware of that."

"Well, that's the one you should watch. Also someone snapped a photo of you two when you met the other week. I don't like this! She's trying to implicate Drex in the video and she compared you two. Like she made it seem like your relationship with her was toxic."

Nathan was quiet for a few moments. He sounded so tired, I wondered if he'd gone to sleep on me.

"Nathan, are you still with me?"

"Yeah. I'm here. I was looking up that interview."

"You can find it on Nessa B's blog. Anyway, I wouldn't wish anyone to get abused or assaulted. She did seem scared on the video on her Instagram profile. Maybe she's just being cautious."

"My head hurts. I don't know what's going on. But I will say this. There was toxicity in my relationship with Autumn. I probably didn't help because I bent over backwards to make sure she was happy. Nadia would tell you that I went way overboard. But nothing seemed to make Autumn happy. I hope you know I respect women and human beings period. I would never put my hands on someone."

"I know that, Nathan. I'm in your corner. And I will tell you what I told my boys earlier, it will all work out. What someone may be meaning for your harm, God will turn that thing around for your good."

Nathan chuckled. "Preach. That's what I needed to hear. I don't think I've been this out of sorts since my injury."

"I love you."

"I love you too, babe. Sleep tight."

When I ended the call, I sat up in bed, my mystery novel forgotten as I tried to wrap my mind around the woman at the center of the storm.

I prayed God would give her a change of heart. Noah had two fathers. The one he'd always known and the one that wanted to get to know him.

Chapter Eight

Today was the day. Noah was coming to Nathan's house. It'd been a long three weeks after Autumn's very public reveal, but God heard our prayers. Candace mentioned to me that Autumn might have wanted to heal from her wounds. That could have been true, but then why show them to the world from her IG profile.

Autumn struck me as a woman who craved attention.

Nathan insisted I be at the house when Noah arrived. I understood his mother and Nadia wanting to meet him, but me being there felt like too much. Plus, if I was really being honest, I didn't want to be around Autumn. Still, I left the salon early, checked on the boys and headed over to Nathan's house.

My heart went out to Noah who was so young and probably not understanding what was going on. He had to miss Drex and now he was meeting a new man, a person who was yet to be revealed as his father. We had all talked about how it would be best to gradually introduce everyone to Noah over time. Once Noah became used to everyone, then he would be told about his father situation. With him being young and Drex remaining in the picture, we prayed the transition would go well for him.

So, I sat on the couch next to Monica with Nadia on the other side. Nathan paced the floor, rubbing his hands across his head. When the doorbell rang, we all jumped in surprise. I prayed the nervous energy would dissipate so Noah would not be afraid. Children could pick up on energy.

Nathan answered the door. From where I sat on the couch, my eyes fell on Autumn first. Her face was covered with large shades and her sandy colored hair flowed around her face. She wore a yellow dress that fell above her knees, accentuating her curves in all the right places. Next to her stood a young boy whose head reached her hip. He had his arms wrapped around what appeared to be a stuffed animal in front of him.

"Hey, Noah." Nathan's voice was hoarse with emotion. "It's good to meet you. I'm a friend of your dad. Come on in."

Noah looked up at Nathan. He smiled, showing off dimples and chipmunk cheeks. My heart melted at the sight of him as he walked into the living room. He twisted his head side to side observing the room, and then stopped in the middle of the room at the sight of us. He turned to look at his mother and then back to us.

Nathan took that moment to introduce us. "This is my mother. My sister and my fiancée."

The boy took his time looking at all of our faces. When his big brown eyes, looking so much like Nathan, rested on me, I smiled back.

He asked. "What's a fiancée?"

Everyone laughed, and Nathan looked at me. "She and I will be getting married. Become husband and wife."

I looked at Nathan, warmed by his explanation and the look of joy on his face. I peered over at Autumn who, despite still wearing shades, also seemed to be facing Nathan's direction too. I wondered how she felt about the way Nathan introduced me to her son.

I'm not sure why I cared.

Next to me Monica twisted her hands in her lap like she wanted to reach out and touch Noah but restrained herself. I could feel her shaking next to me. I reached out and placed my hands on hers.

Under her breath, Monica said, "He looks just like him."

She was right. I'd seen the boy in photos, but up close he really did look like Nathan. There were photos at his parent's house that showed Nathan as a little boy. Noah could have easily been swapped out. I glanced over at Autumn who, despite being inside the house, continued to wear shades. It was a wonder to me how Autumn nor Drex didn't see the resemblance.

On the other side of Monica, Nadia was unusually silent. I'd never been around Nathan's sister when she didn't dominate the conversation with her strong vocal cords. I glanced around Monica and noticed Nadia attempting to wipe her eyes as she looked at Noah.

If Noah noticed the emotions in the room, he didn't seem to be fearful. He bounced on the chair with his stuffed companion next to him. Up close, I could now see it was a bear dressed in a basketball jersey and shorts. The bear's paws were connected to a fabric basketball. I imagined that had to be a gift from Drex, encouraging Noah's love for the game.

For the next few minutes, Nathan and mainly Monica chatted with Noah, who was full of questions about various things in the living room, including family photos.

"Who are these boys?" Noah asked.

I looked at the photo Noah was pointing at and smiled. I forgot Nathan had a photo of my boys in the living room too. He added it not too long after our engagement. Since the boys were often at the house, it seemed like a good thing to make them feel welcome.

Nathan said, "Those are Tangie's sons. They're pretty big. See these two? They're twins. Martin and Mark."

"They look alike, but they are wearing different clothes." Noah commented.

"Yes, and this is Tangie's youngest boy, Drake. He's on the robotics team at his school."

Noah clapped his hands. "Robots. I want to play with robots."

Nathan grinned. "We might introduce you to some of our robots at the school one day."

I appreciated Nathan introducing my boys to Noah. We still hadn't told them about the existence of Nathan's son. It would be a shock to them, but I knew my boys would embrace Noah.

At that moment, Monica, now more comfortable, asked, "Noah, do you want milk and cookies?" Monica had baked chocolate chip walnut cookies, one of Nathan's favorites.

Autumn had been sitting quietly, so still, that I looked over at her every few minutes to make sure she was still breathing. Behind the dark glasses, I couldn't tell what she was thinking. The moment Monica suggested milk and cookies, Autumn shifted forward as if she wanted to protest.

Monica asked, "These cookies do have nuts. Does Noah have any allergies?"

Autumn started to shake her head, but then spoke out loud, "No."

"Good." Nathan's mother held out her hands to Noah and gave Autumn a look that indicated she better not protest. Monica had missed out on being this boy's grandmother all these years. And though no one was revealing the elephant in the room, I knew Nathan's mother intended to relish this moment.

Nathan followed his mother and son into the kitchen leaving me and Nadia.

Nadia, who had remained quiet, took the opportunity to address Autumn. "I hope you are doing well, Autumn."

She faced Nadia. "I am."

It'd been a few weeks since her video was posted, but now I saw why she still wore the shades. The deep bruising was gone around the side of her face, but there appeared to be a scar.

"Did Drex really hit you?"

Nadia was always full of surprises, but her question still had me twisting my head to turn around and look at her. Maybe it wasn't such a good idea to bring this up with Noah in the next room.

Autumn ripped her shades off her face. As expected, her eyes flashed anger and contempt. "I do not want to talk about this while my son is here."

"But you were okay sharing your ordeal with the whole world on your Instagram profile. You know that stuff stays on the internet forever."

"I deleted the post." Autumn snapped. "I was upset that night."

"Mmm. You may have deleted it, but plenty of media outlets reposted the video on their accounts. It isn't going away. I don't appreciate you spreading lies about my brother."

Autumn frowned. "What are you talking about?"

Nadia started to rise from the couch.

Sensing Nadia had been waiting for this moment to confront Autumn, I interrupted. "Nadia is probably referring to your interview with Nessa B. Can we talk about this another time?"

Nadia stood. "No, she doesn't get to destroy my brother again. You left him hanging at the worst time of his life, coming between him and his friend."

Autumn stood. "For your information, they weren't that great of friends. Drex came on to me."

"And you were more than willing to be with him and bring baby boy along too."

Both women were walking towards each other. I jumped up and hissed, "Stop it. Remember today is about Noah getting to know Nathan. We don't need any drama."

Nadia had the sense to step back first, realizing she was going to mess things up for her brother. She turned around and left, leaving me standing next to Autumn, the last person I wanted to be left alone with.

"Thank you," Autumn said.

I turned and looked at her. "I know as a mother we want to do what's best for our children. I'm glad you made this happen, making sure Noah meets Nathan and his family."

Autumn nodded. "Of course. Plus, I needed everyone to know they were wrong about me."

"Wrong about you? What do you mean?"

"Everyone paints me as the bad person, like I just up and left Nathan. I was with him when he got hurt and I would have stayed with him, but he pushed me away. I would have never gone to Drex if Nathan hadn't stopped letting me in. He does that when he's hurt or feeling sorry for himself. He will push you away."

I stared at Autumn, not really sure how to respond to her statement. "Are you saying he let you go?"

She shrugged. "Like I said, he was feeling sorry for himself. Depressed, I guess. With his injury, his world had crashed down on him. He wanted me to move on without him. So I did. But it hurt me to walk away more than anyone will know."

Before I could ask any more questions, Nathan walked back in with Noah holding his hands.

Father and son were smiling.

I peered over at Autumn who for the first time since she'd arrived had lost her sour look. A genuine smile crossed her face.

Something akin to pain exploded in my chest as I watched the exchange between Nathan and Autumn.

Autumn's words still stung. These two had loved each other once. And they had a son together.

Was this a game changer for me and Nathan?

After everyone left, it was just me and Nathan. It had grown late and I hadn't seen my boys since the morning, but I knew they could fend for themselves.

Nathan came up behind me as I cleaned his kitchen. He put his arms around me and for a minute, I relaxed in his arms. "How do you feel?" I asked him.

He stepped back. "I don't know. So much is going on in my head. I feel happy meeting him today and I'm kind of sad that he left. We could have used more time."

"Did Autumn tell you when you can get together again? I'm assuming she will allow regular visits until more legal arrangements can be made."

"I'm trying to ease into bringing in a lawyer. She's in Charlotte now and has a house not too far from here."

I had that familiar creepy feeling. "When did she make the move?"

"Not too long after her and Drex split, she moved back here. She was staying with her aunt for a while."

"She's from this area?"

Nathan yawned. "Yes, she grew up around here. I didn't know her back then but that's how we..."

"Got together," I finished for him.

Nathan glanced at me, his eyes weary. "Yes, it was something we had in common."

I nodded, not really wanting to hear anymore. It could have been the green-eyed monster coming to bite me.

More like Autumn's words.

"We talked a little while you all were in the kitchen. Nadia had a few words and I thought her and Autumn were going to have a confrontation."

Nathan frowned. "Really? I knew something was up when Nadia practically stomped into the kitchen. So you and Autumn talked?"

"Yes, she had a different perspective on how your relationship ended."

"What?"

"She thinks you pushed her away after your injuries. That you let her go. She feels like people think bad about her going to be with Drex." I peered at Nathan to see his reaction. I expected disgust or anger, but instead he looked contemplative.

"Nathan?"

He rolled his head around as if to release tension. "She could be right. I did push her away. It wasn't like she wasn't supportive when I got injured. She encouraged me, but after the doctor told me I pretty much couldn't play anymore on my ankle, I wasn't a good person to be around."

"But you certainly didn't push her towards Drex?"

"I knew Autumn. I knew what she wanted. She wanted me back on the court. But that miracle wasn't going to happen. I wanted her to move on, but the last person I expected it to be with was Drex. We were friends."

"Well, it's good that everything is working out. That you and Drex can work together on being there for Noah."

"That may not be possible."

My mouth dropped open. "What do you mean?"

"Autumn still hasn't confirmed, but she hinted that Drex could have been the one to hit her. She seems really scared about him being around her and Noah."

"Okay. Well, why isn't she bringing him up on charges?"

"Fear, I guess. I'm going to talk to him."

"Should you be doing that? I mean Drex probably isn't going to be happy about you accusing him."

"I know, but Noah doesn't need to be around a man that would be violent against a woman."

"Did Noah indicate that he saw something?"

"I tried to ask him about Drex, but he seemed to not want to talk about him. That has to mean something."

"You think Noah saw Drex hit his mother?"

"I don't know. I just know that what me and Drex talked about might not work. He can't protect Noah by harming his mother. Yes, I know he has every right to be angry with her. But so do I."

I could see Nathan's point, but something felt off to me. He seemed a little too protective of Autumn. Or was he just being this way to protect his son. I wasn't sure, especially now that Nathan seemed to be painting Autumn in a different light.

We sat for a long time. Silence usually was comforting around Nathan, but I had questions swirling. It reminded me of the night Nathan asked me to marry him. I couldn't give him an answer that night. Doubt had consumed me.

I felt that overwhelming sense again as if I was on the verge of losing something. The ringtone on my phone indicated I had a notification. I picked up the phone and read the message. It was a reminder about rescheduling the wedding dress appointment.

Over the past few weeks, I kept putting off the appointment. I even canceled the cake tasting appointment I'd set up for Nathan and myself. Earlier today he'd introduced me to his son as his fiancée, but there had been essentially no discussion about the wedding.

I cleared my throat. "It sounds like you have a lot to get sorted. This thing with Drex and I know you want regular visits with Noah. I think we should postpone the wedding."

Nathan opened his mouth several times like a fish gasping for air. His face morphed into a few emotions finally landing on being perplexed. "Postpone?"

"Yes. Don't you think what's important now is Noah?"

Nathan shut his eyes, squeezing them tight. "I guess so. Tangie, are you sure?"

"I want to support you getting to know your son. Yes, I'm sure."

Even as I said those words, I wasn't really sure. My overly cautious mindset had kicked in. In the back of mind, I had this sense that Nathan was too good to be true. But this was about so much more. I needed to know how this was all going to play out.

My concern was more about the exchange between Nathan and Autumn earlier. With a son together, there was a bond between them forever.

Drex had been a factor, coming in between them four years ago. I couldn't help but wonder how I was going to be able to hold on to Nathan's love when his first fiancée was back in his view.

Chapter Nine

Beulah had become like my second mother. It was my day off from the salon, and I felt like I needed to see her today. The look of hurt on Nathan's face about postponing the wedding kept me awake all night. But I felt it was best. He needed to make up time with his son. And as far as I could tell, there was no plan of action from Autumn. She held off on letting Nathan see his son after dropping a bombshell on him.

Planning a wedding now wasn't the right time.

At least that's what I kept telling myself.

I was sitting in Beulah's kitchen on a Monday. Traditionally, the salon was always closed on Mondays since we worked long days on Saturday. I still did a few clients' hair during the week, but last week I worked more than usual. I'd always been a braider, even before I received my cosmetology license, and I had insisted Crown of Beauty also cater to women with natural hair. Usually I did one to two braid jobs at the most, but last week, I did four. That was a record for me.

Candace noticed and asked how I was doing. She had stopped asking about wedding planning and I never told her that I decided to stop. Candace was my maid of honor and we hadn't even selected her dress yet. Nor did I have a wedding dress. It was pretty obvious nothing was going on and it had become a sore spot with me.

In some ways, I was upset with myself because I'd work myself into believing I had a second chance to love again. All my old insecurities had come back with a vengeance, and I wasn't sure if I could move forward. Not with *that* woman in the picture. Autumn had invaded our lives and she wasn't going away. I wanted Nathan to have a relationship with his son, but I didn't see how I could co-exist with Autumn.

I'd been sitting staring out at the back patio in Beulah's kitchen when I became aware of her return. I'd been grateful but often worried about the exuberant woman who wore her silver hair cropped short. Despite being tied to her home, she dressed fashionably. Today, she wore a leopard skin kimono that reached down to her sandal-clad feet.

"How is Harold doing?"

Beulah pulled out the chair, breathing hard. "He will be fine. The nurse gave him something to sleep. He just gets so agitated sometimes."

Now I felt bad about bothering her as I watched her clasp and unclasp her fingers together, like she was trying to figure out what to do.

Beulah's husband had dementia, one of the reasons why she gave up being at the salon. She wanted to be home to be around him. Unfortunately, he was deteriorating fast and Beulah was against putting him in a nursing home. The problem was it was taking a toll on her own health. A full-figured woman most of her life, I noticed Beulah's face seemed slimmer and she'd lost weight. That was eye-opening to me because I remembered my mom taking that same turn.

"Are you okay, Beulah? You are taking care of yourself, right?"

She waved her hand, hints of the old Beulah returning to her tired face. "Child, I'm good. It's just hard to see Harold this way. I've known that man since I was fifteen years old. We've been married forty-three years." She sniffled. "I know he's not going to be around forever. Neither will

I. But I cherish these moments so much even though they are hard. It's that through sickness and health vow."

I swallowed. I wasn't making it to the altar any time soon to say those vows. In a way, I felt like I was failing already.

Beulah touched my hand. "How are you? I haven't seen you in some time. Not since the bridal shop. I understand from Candace that Nathan has met his son."

I cleared my throat, which seemed to have a lump now. "Yes, I met him too. He's adorable and he's Nathan at that age. Nathan's mom and sister met him too. We're taking it slow. Noah, that's his name, doesn't know that Nathan is his real dad yet."

"That's smart. Getting him used to the family. He's young though, right?"

"Four years old and so smart. Very articulate. He reminds me of Drake at that age."

"Oh, yes, Drake. Now your little man is going to grow up to be some kind of scientist or engineer. I can see it."

I beamed. I felt the same way. My boys, all of them, made me so proud.

"So, I know when you come to see me that something serious is going on. How are you handling Noah's mother?"

I breathed in deep, closing my eyes. Like my mother, Beulah was a mind reader. "I postponed the wedding."

Beulah's eyes widened. "Why would you do that? I know that day at the bridal shop Nathan's sister suggested you should. She wasn't really being very supportive."

I sighed. "She's overprotective of her brother."

"Overprotective or not, I don't think you should put your life with Nathan on hold. He embraced your boys and all of them love him. I know Noah is a surprise element, but you can take him in and love him like your own son."

I shook my head. "It's not that. I accept Noah. I would love to be a part of his life, but I just don't know about his mother. Not confirming the paternity of her son, she has made everything so complicated. Do you keep up with the news? I know you don't really do social media."

"No, but Candace showed me the video. Someone hit this woman. She's married or was married to this basketball player. They're getting a divorce. Did he do this? The man must have been mad about losing his son."

"Drex Armstrong. He claims he didn't touch her. But the night she supposedly was hit, he'd been to her house trying to see Noah. He came by to talk to Nathan. They had worked out being there together for Noah. But after this incident, I think Nathan thinks Drex did something. Now he's pulling back. You know Nadia wants him to get a lawyer and try to get custody of the boy. It's so tricky. Noah, nor the world, knows about his paternity. I just feel like things are too complicated right now. So I told Nathan we should postpone. He seemed really hurt by it and I wonder if I did the right thing."

Beulah nodded. "Well, he has to know you're looking out for him. A wedding is a lot of work and it sounds like you haven't been able to get back to it. My question for you is are you really just postponing it?"

I looked down at the ring. I knew what Beulah was asking me, but I looked at her. "What do you mean?"

Beulah eyed me. "Tangie, you didn't even say yes at first. You had to think about it. Are you sure you want to get married? Especially now that this woman is in the picture. Didn't you say Nathan had been engaged to her?"

I nodded. "Yes. She told me he pushed her away. It sounded like she would have stayed with him even after his injuries. I mean Nathan lost his career, but he was a shrewd businessman. It wasn't like he would go broke. I just always thought she wanted the prestige of being a basketball player's wife."

Beulah cocked an eyebrow at me. "You don't think that's the case? She did go after Nathan's fellow player and they did get married."

I leaned my head back looking up at the ceiling. Beulah recently had her ceiling painted and a large white ceiling fan spun slowly. I turned my attention back to Beulah's concerned face. "I don't know what to think. I just know I've not been this confused in a long time. I feel like I'm trying to do the right thing, but in the back of my mind, I'm wondering if I'm messing up. Am I pushing Nathan away? He looked so hurt."

"Honey, did you discuss it with him or did you make the decision? You know even before you get married, it pays to talk about things. Harold and I didn't talk about a lot of things. He and I always had similar expectations. For a while there, when we were trying to conceive a child, we didn't talk about it. He blamed himself and sometimes me. I blamed myself and wondered if it was on him.

Finally, we talked about it and went to the doctor. Found out we'd been double crossed. Harold got hurt in Vietnam and had no idea his injury would affect him. I always had problems with my cycle. Discovered it was called endometriosis later on. We had to talk through whether we wanted children in another way. We decided together that the two of us were enough and we would pour into other people's children. Have you and Nathan discussed family arrangements? You are still young, and it's still possible for you to have a child."

"I've thought about it. He and my boys get along so well, but I figured he would want a child of his own. I've always wanted a girl. But no, we haven't talked about it. Nathan just became a part of our unit. Sometimes it feels like he's been there the whole time. I know he has a separate relationship with Martin, Mark and Drake."

"I can see how him not knowing he had a child would bring disruption. And that child's mother is a factor. But are you thinking she's going to interfere in your marriage? Would you think Nathan would even allow that?"

I shrugged. "He introduced me to Noah as his fiancée. I just... I don't know. There was this look between him and Autumn, and it just got to me. I wasn't jealous or I don't know, maybe I was. But it changed things. This was a woman he loved and was going to marry. She's a beautiful woman."

Beulah protested. "And so are you. You are a businesswoman and a single mother raising not one but three African American sons. You know the world brings so much difficulty on them. Tangie, I believe Nathan sees your beauty and your strength. Right now, he needs you."

"I'm not going anywhere. I just don't think us getting married is the thing to do."

"You had vows before with your first husband."

"I know. And I will take those vows seriously with Nathan if..."

"If?" Beulah looked at me. "Are you doubtful that Nathan wants to get married now? Tangie, you should talk to him and not be so rash."

"You think I'm pushing him away. That I will push him right into Autumn's arms."

"Is that what you want?"

"I want what's best for Noah."

Beulah shook her head. "It's okay to want to be happy, Tangie. Pray. God didn't place Nathan in your life just to snatch him away and send him back to another woman."

Tears flooded my eyes. "But it's happened to other women. Relationships don't always work out. And don't forget I did lose my first husband. He was snatched away, Beulah. I barely had a chance to say goodbye."

Beulah patted my hand. "Fear comes from the enemy. We don't know God's plans. All we can do is trust Him. Let God be your guide here. Don't let Tangerine Nelson get in the way of what He has in store for you. Pray. And talk to Nathan. Will you do that?"

I nodded, unable to speak.

"Tangie, I know things are difficult, but you make sure you hold on to your love. If anything, you and Nathan need each other now more than ever. If you are feeling some type of way about this woman, don't think it's just jealousy. It could be the Lord trying to warn you. You may have to be the eyes that see something Nathan may not see. He's trying to adjust to being a father. You look out for him."

I heard everything Beulah was saying. That's why I came to her today. Sometimes God placed people in your lives to set you straight. My mother was that person for a long time. I didn't want to push Nathan away. I loved him. Now I just needed to get over my insecurities and make sure we were still going to be a couple.

Chapter Ten

I woke to the sound of the doorbell ringing. I shook my head trying to shake off the nap that had overtaken me. I didn't realize I was so exhausted. I continued working long hours at the salon. Today being Saturday had been especially brutal. Candace insisted I take off and get some rest. Despite talking to Beulah, I still had not had a conversation with Nathan. We'd talked less frequently than usual the past week, and he seemed distant on the phone.

Maybe he was pushing me away.

I was happy that he'd been visiting with Noah more often. But he still hadn't let go of his thoughts on Drex. In fact, the story had picked up steam on the news. No charges had been filed, but Drex had gone on social media protesting that he'd done anything to his wife.

Before falling asleep, I'd watched his latest post.

Drex faced his camera phone and spoke to his fans.

"I filed for divorce and she's just trying to throw anything at me to get what she can from me. That prenup she signed will make sure she doesn't get a dime. I don't appreciate her trying to drag my name through the mud. I don't hit women."

I felt like he was being sincere, but there were so many unanswered questions. If he didn't hit Autumn, then who did. It wasn't like she came right out and said he did anything. She just insinuated.

What was the woman hiding?

Too tired to think anymore, a nap had overtaken me.

But the doorbell still persisted. My eyes flew back open.

Who was that?

The twins had left, taking their younger brother with them for a change. I guess everyone could tell I needed the alone time. With the thought that all my children were out of the house, I felt alarmed and panicked. I stumbled from the couch towards the front door, praying it wasn't bad news on the other side.

"Who is it?"

The person who answered back took me by surprise. I wasn't really sure I heard correctly, but I opened the door anyway.

Nadia stood at the door. In all the time I'd been with Nathan, his sister had not graced my doorstep. I was a little puzzled how she found me. Suddenly, I was afraid again. "Is everything okay? Is Nathan okay?"

Nadia waved her hands like she was calming a crazed woman. "Nathan is fine, girl. I know you are surprised to see me, but it was time for me and you to talk."

"Talk."

"Yes, I get the sense that we hit it off wrong. Don't you think so?"

I nodded. I'd tried with Nadia, but I couldn't say the same for her. I was curious why she wanted to do this now. "Come in."

"Did I disturb you?" Nadia asked as she walked into my living room.

I moved around her and picked up the blanket off the couch. I began folding it. "Sorry for the mess. It's been a long day, actually quite a few long days. I came home from the salon and didn't realize how exhausted I was. My boys are out and the house usually isn't this quiet. I guess I fell asleep. Have a seat. Can I get you anything?"

Nadia sat on the chair adjacent to the couch. "No, I'm fine. I know how that feels. My kids are all out of the house now. I always dreamed of an empty nest, but it's different. The quiet is something to get used to and to cherish."

I sat on the couch and folded my arms. "What did you want to talk about?"

"Nathan and I talked. He mentioned you postponed the wedding. I know I suggested that to you the day we were at the bridal shop, but I was wrong."

I frowned. "I'm sure you feel like I'm not the ideal woman for your brother. I do come with a full package."

Nadia shook her head. "I was never against my brother marrying you. You have good boys, Tangie. I've been around them enough to see that you have done a wonderful job as a single mother. You're an accomplished businesswoman too. You should know Nathan mentioned your first husband to me."

I froze. I didn't talk about Christian much. Nathan was curious about him because Drake kept photos of his father in his bedroom.

"I know about loss, Tangie. I also lost my first husband as well."

I tilted my head. "I never knew that."

"No, like you, I don't talk about it much. People in my family tend to think of me as the woman on marriage number three. But I didn't get there by chance. My first husband and I were high school sweethearts. We were on and off a lot and my family didn't always understand, but he was my first love. My first three children are with him. I remember the years of raising them without their father. It was brutal, having to shove down my feelings and make sure they were cared for. Now I made the mistake of marrying the wrong person the second time and we all paid the price for my mistake."

"You and Steven seem good."

Nadia genuinely smiled. "I like to think so. Third time is the charm, they say. Steven and I have a solid friendship, something I highly value in a relationship. But I didn't come here to talk about me. I wanted to talk about you and Nathan."

"I'm just giving him time to get to know his son."

Her eyes widened. "You're a good woman. I'm sure Nathan appreciates that. My brother hasn't fallen in love that often in his life. But when he does, he falls so hard and every single time he's been disappointed. The last one... Well, Autumn probably was his biggest disappointment. She let him down first by breaking up with him after he was injured, but to pawn his child off on another man. That was the ultimate betrayal."

"I agree. It's a despicable thing to do to him and her son. But she told me Nathan pushed her away, and Nathan confirmed it. Autumn probably should have confirmed Noah's paternity."

Nadia shouted, "Confirmed." She lowered her voice. "Let's think this through. I believe Autumn is trying to control the narrative here. She's already gotten to my brother. I need you to recognize that Autumn had to be seeing Drex long before Nathan was even injured."

I wasn't a math person, but I gave Nadia my attention. "Okay. You figure that how?"

"By what she's saying. She says that she didn't start messing with Drex until after Nathan pushed her away. Then she had to know that child, based on his age, was clearly Nathan's. She was still obligated to tell him."

I nodded in agreement. "Or the other scenario is she was already cheating with Drex behind Nathan's back, and then he got injured. She was already pregnant for some time, but because she was sleeping with both men, she figured it could have been Drex or Nathan's"

"Exactly, which still puts her in the wrong light to me. Either way she tries to paint herself, Autumn is still trying getting around what she did. I get sick about it. You know I'm considerably older than Nathan. I was almost ten years old when he was born. There was a boy born in between us, but he was stillborn. Mama didn't try again or at least that I knew of.

"Nathan is my Mama's heart, her miracle baby. She's been talking about Noah the past few days. It breaks my heart that Nathan has to do all of this scheduling just so he can see his own son. Tangie, my brother doesn't need any more disappointments in his life. I'm sorry that I told you to postpone the wedding. Please don't."

I looked down at my hands, staring at the diamond as it caught the sunlight streaming through my living room windows. "The wedding planning has been intense and like you said, Nathan is trying to work through seeing his son. Autumn came out of the blue with her announcement, and I'm ashamed to say it knocked me for a loop. I'm not sure how she factors into our lives now."

Nadia smacked her hands on her thighs. "Surely you don't think Nathan is interested in her?"

I stood, my emotions wracking my body so that I could no longer remain still. "I don't doubt your brother's love for me. But she was the woman he loved and they have a child together. They are going to be spending more time together. It would be impossible for Nathan to not feel something towards her. He was angry, but her story has softened his feelings."

Nadia bellowed making me almost jump out of my skin. "She's playing with him. She sees that he's doing well despite not playing on the court. I'm sure you've seen Drex on social media. He's not giving her a dime. I'm pushing Nathan to get a lawyer. He doesn't need to be caught up in trying to go with her schedule. He needs custody of his son."

I spun and looked at her. "Is that wise right now? Noah still doesn't know Nathan is his real father. If this goes into the court system, won't news about Noah's paternity get out?"

Nadia stood and walked over to me. "That's a risk. Look, I know this is moving fast, but Nathan needs to get custody of his son. Autumn used that boy to get fame and fortune as Drex's wife. As far as I'm concerned, she's unfit. She clearly came back here to try to wiggle her way back into my brother's life and she's dangling his son in front of him."

I started to open my mouth to protest, but Nadia held up her hand to stop me.

"I know how much Nathan loves you and your boys. He can't lose you. I think it would break him. You and your sons are his family. I'm sorry for being too overprotective of my brother. I realize now that he has what he needs in you. He needs you now more than ever."

I stared at Nadia for a moment, the realization of the real reason for her visit dawned on me and I stepped back. "Are you saying this to me because you know me and Nathan getting together would help his chances of getting his son?"

"No. What kind of woman do you think I am?"

I tilted my head. "You have to admit it would be to his benefit to have a stable family."

"Tangie, before all of this happened, you and Nathan were going to get married regardless. He asked you to marry him long before he knew he had a son. I'm asking you to stick by him. I know Autumn presents a difficulty because of the way she's gone about this, but she should not be able to mess with you and my brother's happiness. She had her chance and she lost it. I'm saying make sure she's aware of that. Stand by my brother."

Though doubts swirled in my head, Nadia made sense. Nathan and I had not set out to find love, but love found us and placed us together. Marriage came with unseen obstacles of all kinds.

I knew this was one time where I needed to put my faith into action.

Chapter Eleven

With Beulah, Candace and now Nadia urging me on, I went back to Lenora's Bridal Shop. I still hadn't talked to Nathan. Instead, I reached out and rescheduled the dress fittings. My maid of honor, Candace, and all my bridesmaids' lavender dresses were set to go to the seamstress for fittings.

From the previous appointment, I asked Lenora to pull the last dress I'd tried on. The strapless dress with the lace felt like it belonged on my body. I couldn't see that the last time because my head was cluttered with Autumn's bombshell announcement. Now the dress spoke to me. I could see myself walking down the aisle towards Nathan.

I found my dress.

That was all I had for now.

The one appointment I had not canceled was the pre-marital counseling session. Since Nathan nor I seemed to be able to find time to talk, I figured this would be a start. I had high hopes that we would walk away with blessings on a final wedding date.

Or maybe this would be more than a postpone-ment.

We didn't arrive together at Victory Gospel. I used the excuse that I would be arriving from the salon. Nathan had finished his day's work at The Lab hours ago. When I entered the pastor's sec-retary's office, I saw Nathan sitting on the couch outside Reverend Freeman's office. I stood in the doorway, transfixed by him like usual. I hadn't seen him in a few days.

His head was bent, face intense as he typed on his phone. I wondered who had his rapt attention.

My conversation with Nadia rang in my ears.

I know how much he loves you and your boys. He can't lose you. I think it would break him.

Nathan must have sensed my presence. He looked up and placed his phone inside his coat pocket.

I looked to my right. Reverend Freeman's door was closed and his secretary wasn't at her desk.

We were alone.

I took a deep breath, bolstering my legs to continue forward. "I didn't mean to interrupt."

He stood. Even though I wasn't a short woman by any means, it always felt like he towered over me a bit. "It was my lawyer. He reached out to Autumn today. She's not happy, but I'm not sure what she expected."

"Your sister told me you were going after custody."

He raised an eyebrow. "You and Nadia talked?"

"Yeah, she surprised me. I have always known how protective she is of her baby brother."

Nathan scoffed. "My sister is a mess but I love her. She acts like she's taking my mother's place sometimes."

Knowing how Nadia liked to boss her brother, I grimaced. "She means well."

Reverend Freeman's office door opened and he stepped out and smiled. "Nathan. Tangie. Come on in."

Nathan held out his arms and I walked in first. We both sat in the two leather chairs in front of Reverend Freeman's massive oak desk. I'd been in this office only one time and that was years ago when I first joined Victory Gospel. Reverend Freeman liked to have sessions with new members, helping them discover their talents and where they could fit in. It was here that I received instructions about the bible study for single women and I'd met friends, a few who'd gone on to get married.

"So, I hear you have postponed the wedding. It's good you came to see me today. I appreciate you keeping the appointment. Are there some things you want to talk through?"

I peered at Nathan, who caught my eye.

Nathan cleared his throat. "What we tell you is confidential?"

"Absolutely."

"Good, because I want to protect a little boy. I've learned... we've learned together that I have a son."

Reverend Freeman raised an eyebrow. "Please tell me more."

Nathan explained about Noah and his past relationship with Autumn. He told the pastor about Drex and the current divorce. "I'm in the process of seeing if I can get custody of Noah, at least some form of joint custody so that I'm not always at the whims of Autumn deciding when I can see my son."

Reverend Freeman nodded. He'd been jotting down some notes. "That makes sense. Who decided to postpone the wedding?"

I raised my hand. "That would be me. I had good intentions. I felt like Nathan had been hit with some life changing news and he needed time to get to know his son."

Reverend Freeman asked, "Is that the only reason for your hesitancy?"

I had not talked to Nathan about this. I wished I'd followed Beulah's admonitions to talk to him. Now, I had no choice but to tell my truth. I looked at Nathan, whose eyes held concern. "If I'm being honest, I'm grateful Autumn came forward to tell Nathan about his son. But I'm wondering if she would have ever told him if the boy hadn't gotten sick. She talked to me a few weeks ago and I got the impression she wanted to share her side of things. Anyway, I'm not sure what to think of her."

I turned to Nathan. "I want us to be together, but Autumn is a concern."

Nathan shook his head. "She shouldn't be. If you think I still have feelings for her, I promise you, I don't. I feel like I walk a tightrope with her. Noah still doesn't know I'm his father. He still thinks Drex is his dad and he's four years old. He doesn't understand. I'm trying to be cool."

That's when it dawned on me. "You feel like if you show anger or if you are not cooperative, that she will take Noah away?"

"Absolutely. I don't trust Autumn. I know she says she started being with Drex after I was injured, but I heard too many stories that say different. I believe she didn't know whose baby she was carrying. It's true I pushed her away, but it's because she kept hounding me. She was the one who didn't want to believe my injury couldn't miraculously heal. I remember praying and praying about it. I was so down because I felt like God wasn't hearing me."

Reverend Freeman leaned forward. "God hears all of our prayers. We don't understand His plans for us, but it's for our good. It's to drive us closer to our purpose. While you're not on the court, your Assist Group is doing amazing things. You are one of a few African American men in a profession that doesn't have many like you. I dare say you've made more of impact in the education field than when you were on the basketball court."

"Thank you, Rev. I appreciate that."

"Tangie, you've blossomed since you've joined Victory Gospel Church. I remember the pain you felt when you walked through those doors. God's equipped you to raise three young men. It appears you may have another young boy in the midst. Is that something you are ready for?"

I smiled. "Absolutely. Noah is an adorable boy and I can't wait for my boys to meet him."

"So can we get your wedding date back on the books?"

Nathan and I exchanged glances. The heat in his eyes warmed my soul. "Of course. If the original date is still available, I say let's keep it."

"Excellent. Let's make this happen July 28 as planned. As husband and wife, you will have to weather many storms. Let what's going on right now be a lesson in how you do this marriage thing together. I want you to talk to each other. Communication is where marriages start to break down. Learn to be honest with one another."

We shook hands with Reverend Freeman and walked out together.

Nathan stopped me when we reached my car. He cupped his hand around my elbow and turned me towards him. "I'm sorry, Tangie, if you felt like I'd been giving mixed signals. You are the only woman for me. I knew back then that Autumn wasn't the kind of woman for me. She hung around basketball players on purpose trying to see which one of us she could snag. I pushed her away back then because it was easier. She wasn't helping me move past my injuries. I felt like more of a failure."

"I'm sorry too. I trust you. I know you love me, and I'm here to support you and Noah. I prefer not to have confrontations because that brings out a side of me I don't like. But I will deal with Autumn. She won't get between us."

"Good, that's what I want to hear. Now I've missed you and I'm hoping we can make up for a lot of lost time."

Chapter Twelve

Three Months Later

Wedding Day

I really hoped this waterproof mascara held because I was going to mess up my makeup for sure. I eyed my oldest son as he grinned back at me. My arm was hooked inside of his.

"Are you ready, Mama?"

Tears blurred my eyes. Despite the tremble in my body, I smiled. "Yes, just don't make me cry yet."

"I got you, Mama."

The melody of the wedding march guided me forward as my son walked beside me down the aisle. I caught glimpses of people on both sides of me, but my eyes were trained on the man at the end of this walk.

Nathan stood; his eyes locked on mine. The smile on his face just about took me out.

Therefore what God has joined together, let man not separate.

This man was going to be my husband after we exchanged our vows. After everything that happened, we would do this.

Together.

I glimpsed over to see Drake holding on to the newest member of our family. Noah wriggled as he held onto the pillow. Our ring bearer looked so handsome and so much like Nathan.

Reverend Freeman spoke, "Who gives this woman?"

Martin said, "I do." He looked at me and then at Nathan. My soon-to-be husband and eldest shared a head nod before I walked up beside Nathan.

As Reverend Freeman guided us through our vows, the tremble that had been with me for the past few hours began to subside. The sun's rays shone across the sanctuary lighting up the mass of lilacs that adorned the altar. I could feel the presence of God, letting me know He was here in the midst. That all Nathan and I had to do was trust Him.

After months of planning, the ceremony was quick. Before I knew it, Nathan had bent down to kiss me. And I couldn't stop the flow of tears.

This has finally happened.

I almost didn't say yes the first time Nathan asked me to marry him. And my decision to postpone could have easily turned into a cancellation. I was so thankful for the guidance and prayers Nathan and I had received the past few months.

The joy of the wedding ceremony continued into the reception as we were announced to the crowd of family and friends.

Mr. and Mrs. Nathan Chambers.

I hadn't had a chance to see who came to the wedding even though I'd poured over the RSVP list for the past few days. As we made our way through the row of tables to our seats at the front of the reception hall, I glimpsed Drex. He gave a salute to us as we passed by.

Despite the turmoil in the past few months, Nathan and Drex talked to Noah together letting him know he had two fathers who would be there for him. Noah was still getting used to the idea, but he loved spending time with Nathan. And just as I expected, after getting over the initial shock, my sons had embraced Noah too. Drake loved not being the youngest and had taken Noah under his wings pretty much like a big brother.

Once Nathan and I were seated, I looked around the room seeing so many people we loved like Beulah and Candace. Nathan's mother and Nadia.

My eyes fell on a woman I really didn't expect to show up for the wedding. Everyone told me I didn't have to invite her. But something told me I had nothing to fear. My mother always told me to keep your enemies where you could see them. Not that I considered Autumn an enemy. She'd shown the world her true self and I wasn't really bothered by her. I just wanted Noah to feel comfortable and loved. And his mother was who she was, but she loved her son.

Besides, it appeared Autumn had brought a date with her. From where he sat, I could tell he was as tall as Nathan and Drex.

I leaned over to Nathan. "I see Autumn has moved on."

Nathan peered in the direction I was looking. "Yes, Drex mentioned she had a new guy. Barry Sanders. He plays for the Charlotte Hornets."

"He's a brave man." I commented.

"Or a very stupid one." Nathan was uncharacteristically blunt.

But Autumn deserved it.

She had harmed herself hours before her infamous video was posted, and the person who outed her was her own son. Noah had climbed out of bed seeking solace and a glass of water when he heard his mother cries. He thought maybe she walked into the door, but Autumn had purposely used the door to create a story.

Nathan and I found this story out during an innocent conversation with Noah. Since then, Drex had sued Autumn.

The blogger Nessa B also claimed Autumn set up the meeting where she was able to snap a photo of Nathan and Autumn. Her own admission backfired on the blogger making her come off as not very credible. Not that anyone was surprised. Many of Nessa's stories had been revealed to be false. Last I heard, her blog had been taken down and she'd disappeared from social media.

Unfortunately, Noah's paternity did leak to the public, but it didn't affect him. We all made sure of that. The negative effects have mainly haunted Autumn. I'm pretty sure she showed up to our wedding to put on a good public face. She had a lot of rebuilding to do for her reputation.

I wished her well. I truly did.

In the meantime, a judge had awarded full custody of Noah to Nathan, allowing visitation privilege for Autumn as she navigated her legal battles.

My only concern was that Drex remain on the other side of the room. I would show my true colors today if anyone decided to mess with our wedding day.

The DJ interrupted the group conversations. "It's time for the first dance. Mr. and Mrs. Chambers, can you start us off?"

Nathan and I grinned at each other. We'd been waiting for this moment. What others didn't know, not even our boys, is we had been practicing our dance. When we stepped on the dance floor, we were about to blow everybody's mind.

The DJ winked at us; he had the playlist ready to go. Jagged Edge's "Let's Get Married" started playing, and I started swaying my hips. As the hooting and hollering rose around us, Nathan and I grooved, our steps in sync.

Our love forever.

About Tyora Moody

Tyora Moody is the author of **Soul-Searching Mysteries,** which includes **cozy mystery, women sleuth mystery, and mystery romance** under the Christian Fiction genre. Her books include the Eugeena Patterson Mysteries, Serena Manchester Mysteries, Reed Family Mysteries, and the Victory Gospel Series.

When Tyora isn't working for a literary client, she's either loving on her cats, listening to an audiobook or podcast, binge-watching crime shows or Marvel movies, and of course, thinking about the next book. To contact Tyora about reviewing her books or book club discussions, visit her online at TyoraMoody.com.

Also By Tyora Moody

Victory Gospel Shorts
The Replacement Date, #1
Southern Delights, #2
When Love Finds Me, #3
Nobody's Replacement, #4
A Southern Delights Christmas, #5
Holding on to Love, #6

Eugeena Patterson Mysteries
Deep Fried Trouble, #1
Oven Baked Secrets, #2
Lemon Filled Disaster, #3
A Simmering Dilemma, #4
An Unsavory Mess, #5

Serena Manchester Mysteries
Hostile Eyewitness, prequel
Bittersweet Motives, #1
Dangerous Confessions, #2
Waning Innocence, #3

Reed Family Mysteries
Broken Heart, #1
Troubled Heart, #2
Relentless Heart, #3
Faithful Heart, #4
Wounded Heart, #5

Victory Gospel Series
When Rain Falls, #1
When Memories Fade, #2
When Perfection Fails, #3